Following His Heart

Donna Fasano

Copyright © 2014, Donna J. Fasano
Following His Heart
Paperback ISBN 978-1-939000-30-9
eBook ISBN 978-1-939000-31-6

Formatting by the Fairies of BippityBoppityBook.com

Follow the author:
 Facebook – https://www.facebook.com/DonnaFasanoAuthor
Twitter – https://Twitter.com/DonnaFaz
Pinterest – https://Pinterest.com/DonnaFaz

CHAPTER ONE

Up to her elbows in sudsy water, Sara Carson frowned as she watched the heavy baking sheet slip from the counter and bounce off the ancient pipe that ran along the baseboard. Her eyes widened in absolute horror when water from the busted fitting sprayed a forceful, ten-foot arc toward the cooling racks in the center of the room that held the hundreds of perfect, jack-o-lantern-shaped sugar cookies she'd spent hours baking. The mouth-watering aroma of warm vanilla that she'd just paused to savor seemed to swirl and drown in some awful eddy along with the satisfied smile that *had* been on her lips just a moment before.

Without even thinking about it, she dove for the tray—soap bubbles flying everywhere—and wielded it like a shield against the onslaught. Water soaked her blouse and apron and plastered her bangs against her forehead, but the tray redirected the shower for now. Her eyes were wild as she looked around and tried to figure out what to do next. She couldn't continue squatting here for long. Someone needed to run to the utility room and turn off the water at the main valve.

She'd never make her deadline if she didn't save those cookies.

"Cathy!" she yelled. But she knew she would never be heard above the morning news that was blaring in the café next door to her shop. And she didn't dare do the job herself; by the time she reached the water nozzle, every single cookie would be ruined.

She ran a frantic gaze around the kitchen and saw a tea towel over on the island. Wrapped around the fitting, the towel might hold back the water long enough for her to get to the utility room. Sara stretched out her arm, continuing to hold tight to the cookie sheet with her other hand. *Reach*. Oh, for criminy's sake. It was impossible. Too far away.

The water struck the cookie sheet on one corner, shoving it into Sara's face and knocking her off balance. A stream escaped, shooting into the air and landing, dead-center on a full tray of cookies.

"Damn it!" Sara muttered as she twisted back around to block the spray.

By now, her white canvas sneakers were sodden, her toes swimming in the spongy cushion-soles each time she shifted her weight. Her knees and thighs began to ache.

The phone! The thought seeped into her thoughts and sent her scrambling in her back pocket for her cell, but when she let loose of the sheet, it once again smacked her in the forehead and allowed more water to douse her.

"Time for a new plan," she said right out loud, and she reached around, curled her fingers around the pipe until her palm was directly over the leak. She squeezed as tightly as she could. Then with her free hand, she pulled out her phone and called Cathy.

It only rang once.

"Can't talk. The place is packed and I'm short one waitress."

Sweet and soft-spoken were not words anyone would use to describe Cathy, and Sara wasn't surprised that her friend answered so tersely. The woman might own a sharp tongue, but she had a heart of gold and had been one of those rare, you-can-count-on-me kind of friends for a lot of years.

"I'm at the shop. I've got a leak," Sara said, clear panic in her voice.

"Look, the pancakes on the griddle need to be turned. I've got three customers who want to eat their eggs while they're still hot. And the timer's going to go off any second now. I have to be here to pull the biscuits out of the oven."

The Sunshine Grill was Cathy's pride and joy. Open for breakfast and lunch, it had an abundance of loyal locals who frequented the restaurant as well as the throng of boardwalk tourists who flooded the place. When Cathy divorced her husband several years ago, she'd thrown herself into making a success of her establishment. Her customers came first, above all else.

"I'm feeding people here. Can you call Heather?" Cathy asked.

The hypotenuse of their triangle, Heather owned the building and ran The Lonely Loon, the B&B located above Sara's Sweet Shop and The Sunshine Grill.

"She had an appointment this morning. I need you to turn off the water."

Sara heard kitchen noises, the clatter of utensils and porcelain plates, along with the blare of the morning news being broadcast from the television anchored high on the wall in sight of all the customers.

"I'm in the middle of breakfast service, Sara. I need water."

The building had been constructed in the 1920s and the plumbing and wiring were forever failing. Years ago when the first floor had been turned into a restaurant, Heather's mother, The Lonely Loon's proprietor at the time, knew someone on the City Counsel who had grandfathered the plans so that the restaurant could share water pipes with the bed and breakfast. And by some amazing miracle, the woman was able to grease more palms when a portion of the restaurant had been refurbished into an ice cream parlor more than two dozen years ago. The parlor had since been turned into Sara's Sweet Shop—a bakery that supplied local restaurants with delicious pies, cakes, cookies, breads, and other baked goods.

The need to have the plumbing overhauled and the building rewired was often a topic of conversation between Heather, Cathy, and Sara, but they continued to bandage, staple, glue, fold, cinch, and pad the leaky pipes and fixtures until they could decide on the best time, not to mention finding the money, to close down all three businesses in order to do some modernizing.

"We can't shut off the water for a drippy

faucet," Cathy groused. "Wrap a towel around that thing. We'll fix it later."

At that very moment, a small jet of water forced its way between Sara's fingers and struck her under the chin. Icy water ran down her neck and between her breasts, and that's when she lost her temper.

"You get your ass to the utility room right this second," she screamed, "and turn the damn water off!"

Cathy went silent on the other end of the phone for several long seconds. Yelling and cursing wasn't in Sara's makeup. Not normally. But she looked over at her sugar cookies and the thought of all those hours of labor and the cost of ingredients wasted short-circuited all the *niceness* that was in her.

The muscles in Sara's hand and wrist were growing fatigued, and she was just about to give a second shout when she heard her friend's voice.

"Um, hon," Cathy told her, "you're on speaker."

Landon Richards sat at the counter of the The Sunshine Grill, waiting for the short stack of pancakes with a side of brown sugar and cracked pepper bacon he'd ordered from the harried woman behind the counter—"Cathy" machine embroidered onto her bright aqua chef's jacket. No matter how hard he tried, he was unable to avoid eavesdropping on her cell phone conversation. In fact, practically everyone in the restaurant had stopped eating and openly stared at Cathy.

The woman on the other end of the phone groaned.

"I'm sorry, Cath, but I *need* you. Water's shooting everywhere. I can't hold it back much longer. I'm going to lose my cookies."

Pure instinct had Landon standing up and waving to capture Cathy's attention. His family hadn't dubbed him The Answer Man for nothing. He'd spent nearly twenty years solving problems and keeping the family business organized and running smoothly.

"Can I help?" he asked. "Where's the utility room?"

Cathy shook her head. "Oh, I couldn't ask you to do that."

"Ask him!" the frantic voice shouted from the cell. Without waiting for a response, she continued, "Through the kitchen. Make a left. The utility room is the last door on your right. Hurry. *Move* it!"

"This way," Cathy told him. Seemingly in

one smooth motion she disconnected the call, shoved the phone in the back pocket of her jeans, delivered two plates of food to customers sitting at the counter, then waved Landon toward her. "Through there—" she pointed at the door at the back of the kitchen. When he hurried past her, she was already at the sink, filling a large pitcher with water. "Left, then right at the end of the hall. I think the main nozzle is red. Tell Sara to rig up the leak and get the water back on, pronto. Without fresh coffee, my customers will revolt."

"I'm on it." Landon offered her a little salute before starting off on his mission. Then he paused and turned back just in time to see her flipping the pancakes that, he guessed, were to be his breakfast. "Um, where is she? This Sara you were just talking to?"

"Next door. The door to her shop is almost directly across from the utility room. You can't miss it."

The look on his face made Cathy chuckle. "Yes, we share water pipes. It's complicated." The timer on the stove beeped, and Cathy reached for a large oven mitt that touted a huge yellow sun. "Go," she urged. "And when you get back, breakfast is on the house."

The utility room was easy enough to find, and so was the nozzle. Yes, it had been red at one time, but the paint was nearly all peeled off now and gray corrosion encrusted the fixture. He cranked down on the nozzle until it wouldn't turn anymore, then he scanned the gray metal shelving units, plucking off some items he thought Sara would need. A bucket, for sure, he thought. If she was going to toss her cookies, she certainly didn't want to have *that* mess on top of what must be a small flood in her shop. Several old, raggedy towels. A small, blue plastic tool box. And a roll of silver duct tape.

At least semi-armed and ready, he didn't bother trying to close the door behind him. He could come back and do that later. He made his way to the first door across the hall and pushed his way inside. Heady smells both warm and sweet engulfed him, but his mission had him barely noticing.

"Hello?" he called.

"Here. Over here. By the sink."

He didn't have to go far to find her.

"Thanks," she said in a rush. "So much. I was sure I was going to lose my cookies."

Landon set the toolbox on the counter so quickly it *thumped*, then he pulled the towels and tape from the bucket, tossed them next to the toolbox, and shoved the empty bucket directly in front of her.

"Here you go." He slid his hand behind her head and applied the slightest bit of pressure. "Let 'er rip."

She braced both hands on the bucket rim, and for a moment or two, they played a little tug of war; her trying to sit up, and him pressing her down.

Finally, she said, "Stop!"

He blinked and straightened his spine. The look in her vivid green eyes told him she thought he was crazy.

"*What are you doing?*"

"Sorry," he muttered, feeling confused and lifting both hands, palms out. "I was just trying to help. You, ah, you, um..."

The woman looked like she'd just stepped out of the ocean. She was on her knees, her shins and shoes sitting in a pool of water. There wasn't a dry patch of skin or clothing on her. Her hair was stuck to her skull, and the dark makeup around her eyes was smudged, giving her a raccoon-like appearance. A cute raccoon, but a raccoon, nonetheless.

He couldn't hold back his smile, and before he could stop it, a chuckle erupted from his throat. "You are quite a sight."

She reached up and smoothed a self-conscious hand over her head while water dripped from her earlobes, the ringlets at her nape, even from the tip of her nose.

"Yeah, I guess I am. I was just visited by what's known around here as the primitive plumbing monster, and it seems I lost again." She reached out her hand to him. "I'm Sara Carson."

He shook her cool, wet hand. "Landon. Landon Richards."

"Well, thank you for coming to my rescue, Landon. Now how about answering my question." She glanced down at the bucket, then her gaze lifted back to his face. "What was that all about?"

His brow knit together. "But I already told you. I was trying to help."

"By shoving my face in a bucket?"

The question made his frown deepen. "You said you were going to be sick. I heard you clear as day. You said it twice."

Her expression, along with her utter silence, told him that he'd completely bewildered her. So he attempted to explain further.

"You said you were going to... you know, upchuck. Where I come from, we say toss our cookies, not—"

"I said I was going to *lose* my cookies."

She reached out her hand to him, and he heard the sound of sloshing water as he helped her to stand.

"Exactly," he told her, continuing to feel bewildered.

Sara lifted her hands, pointing toward the center of the room with both her index fingers, and he automatically turned to look.

The stainless steel island was covered with cookies. Three six-foot steel racks were filled with cookies, as well. Landon felt the heat of embarrassment creep up his neck. Then he put it together, the luscious scent of butter and vanilla. He should have known as soon as he walked into the kitchen.

He turned to face her.

"I'm not from around here," he told her, the words coming in a rush. "I thought it was some sort of local colloquialism."

She just stared for a moment, and then her mouth twitched with humor. She shook her head and lifted her wet fingers to her lips, but in the end, she couldn't contain her laughter.

Landon watched this sopping woman's shoulders shake, her mascara smudged into black circles beneath her eyes, her hair adhered to her forehead and neck, and for the first time in many months he forgot all about the eerie episodes that had plagued him for so long. He suddenly realized that the dark and disquieting cloud that constantly hovered over him, urging him on in his travels, had dissipated—at least for that one, small minute. He realized he felt feather light inside, and happy, so he did the only thing that felt right; he joined Sara in laughter.

And it felt *wonderful*.

CHAPTER TWO

DISASTERS WERE FUNNY things. They almost always arrived unexpectedly, and like a long-handled rake hiding in a lush, green lawn, they had the ability to knock you out cold. A disaster could so easily turn into life-changing tragedy, as Sara was already well aware. She'd suffered her fair share of hardship, no one could dispute that.

But *thwarting* calamity? Now that had a way of proving what you were made of, what lengths to which you were willing to go in order to protect what meant something to you. She'd been willing to look like a drowned rat in front of a man she'd never met in order to save all those hours of labor she'd put into baking those sugar cookies. And in helping her prevent what would have been a great setback for her, Landon Richards had revealed a lot about himself as well.

He was the kind of person who raced to the aid of strangers. That was a rare trait. Most people didn't want to even know about the trouble of others, let alone get involved. But he'd stepped up and acted without hesitation. The fact that he was even willing to slide a bucket under her face to prevent her from making even more of a mess was clear evidence that he was a good guy who had a great heart.

The whole bucket thing still made Sara grin even now, hours later. Landon had used duct tape and towels and more duct tape to staunch the leak so the water could be turned back on. He'd even helped her mop up the floor. As promised, Cathy had served him a hearty breakfast at no charge, and she'd been happy to do it because his quick reaction enabled her to keep the restaurant open and feed her customers. It was while Landon had been enjoying his breakfast at a table overlooking the boardwalk and the ocean beyond that he'd offered to replace the section of pipe that had been damaged by the baking sheet.

"Really, it's nothing," he'd told both Sara

and Cathy after they'd thanked him half a dozen times. "And please don't offer to pay me again. I'm happy to do it."

"But do you realize how much money you'll be saving us?" Cathy had asked, bringing him a second helping of thick-sliced, crispy bacon and a side of her homemade cinnamon applesauce.

Sara had sat across from him, enjoying a cup of coffee as he ate. "She's right, you know. It would cost hundreds of dollars to have a plumber drop everything and fix this for us."

But the good guy with the great heart had assured them, over and over, that he was happy to help.

"And you're sure you know what you're doing?" Cathy blatantly asked.

"Cathy!" The question had taken Sara aback, so she could only imagine how it had made Landon feel.

"It's okay." He'd offered a good-natured grin. "It's a pertinent question from someone who's relying on that plumbing." Then he'd looked at Cathy. "Yes, I know I can replace the pipe. When you grow up on a farm, you learn how to fix darn near anything."

So that's how, after a quick run to the hardware store, she and Landon ended up back in the sweet shop. Sara stood at the island and wrapped cookies in small cellophane packets as she watched Landon working on the damaged pipe.

"So what brings you to Ocean City?" she asked.

The muscles of his broad back bunched beneath his white t-shirt as he applied pressure to the pipe cutter.

He didn't answer her for the longest time, and then one of his shoulders lifted in a small shrug. "I just had this urge to see the ocean."

Automatically, Sara's gaze lifted to look out the big picture window of her shop. Bright afternoon sunlight sparked and glinted off the blue green water of the Atlantic. She sighed.

"I understand. I feel that urge every day. I never get tired of looking at the water, listening to the waves."

He set the pipe cutter on the floor and glanced up at her. "It is a beautiful sound. I never knew what I was missing."

Sara stopped tying the bow mid-loop. "The way you say that..." She cocked her head. "You've never heard waves before?"

"Nope," he admitted. "Up until a few weeks ago, I hadn't. Well, not that didn't come from a television show or a movie, or something like that. But real pounding against a real shoreline? Huh-uh."

The cookie-packed cellophane bag was momentarily forgotten as she asked, "You said you live on a farm. Where are you from?"

"Kansas."

"Wow. That's, like, a thousand miles away, isn't it?"

He smiled. "Over thirteen hundred, actually. I'm from west of Topeka."

"Did you drive? Or fly?"

"Drove every single mile in my pickup."

"Must have taken you a couple of days," she said. "So you're on vacation?"

His brown gaze slid from hers and he turned to wrestle the cut piece of pipe from the rest of the length. Sara felt a dull pang of regret over nosing into his business.

"I'm sorry," she said. "I shouldn't be pestering you with a bunch of questions when you're trying to work."

"No, it's fine. I don't mind the questions," he told her, his back still to her. "I guess you could call it a vacation. We, uh, sold the family farm recently. My sister just had her second child, and my brother-in-law got a great paying job with the corporation that made the offer on our land. So... I agreed it was the right thing to do. At least, for them." After a moment's pause, he added, "I guess it was right for everyone. Ever since my operation, I'd been feeling...

well, unsettled and... I don't know..." He went quiet, and he finally turned his head to look up at her, chuckling. "I guess saying I'm on vacation is as good an explanation as any."

The hesitant manner in which he'd explained things told Sara that he hadn't wanted to sell the farm. And she wondered what sort of operation he'd had. He looked fit and healthy. The corded muscles of his back sure shouted *strong and able-bodied* to her. Sara moistened her lips, tore her gaze away, and forced herself to focus on packaging the cookies.

The tidbits he'd revealed only made her more curious about him, but delving further into his personal business would have been rude.

"The day after we signed the settlement papers," he continued, "I packed a bag, climbed into my truck, and headed due east."

As he talked, he used some sort of gadget to clean the layers of old paint off the cut edges of the water line.

"I ended up in New Jersey. The sand, the surf, the sunshine. I'd never seen anything so beautiful."

Sara smiled. "Wait a minute, now. Surely you have sunshine in Kansas. That's what helps make all those acres and acres of corn grow, right?"

He laughed. "That's true enough. But near the ocean, the sun feels... different... no, the *air* feels different. You can smell the salt."

"Yeah." She nodded. "I love that tang. Believe it or not, it's stronger some days than others."

"I spent a couple of days there in Atlantic City," he said, grabbing a wad of steel wool and buffing the ends of the pipe, both inside and out. "The casinos were exciting and all, and the boardwalk was great, but the town didn't feel..." He paused for a few seconds before murmuring, "I was going to say *right*. But that sounds a little odd, doesn't it?"

Before she could respond, he continued talking.

"I drove south. Spent some time in Sea Isle City, and Stone Harbor, and a place called Wildwood. I ended up in Cape May. Now that's a cute little town." He reached around for one of the couplings he'd purchased at the hardware store, but it rolled a foot or so away from him.

Sara moved to retrieve it and bent over to place it in his palm. "Cape May's nice. I've been there quite a few times. My mom and I used to go over to look at the Christmas lights when I was a kid."

"Did you ride the ferry?"

His eyes were glittering when he gave her a quick glance, and Sara nodded. The Cape May-Lewes Ferry operated a daily shuttle service across the Delaware Bay.

"Yes, I've ridden it lots of times."

He turned back to his work. "That was an interesting experience. I drove my pickup right onto that boat. That thing is huge."

"People around here love that ferry," Sara said, moving back to the island. "I think it can carry a hundred cars and something close to a thousand passengers at a time across the bay."

Landon whistled. "The trip took about an hour and a half. I saw three light houses, and all sorts of seabirds. I really enjoyed that part of my trip."

He put all the now shiny-clean pieces together like a puzzle. "The dry fit looks great." Then he took them all apart. "So tell me about you. You've lived by the ocean all your life?"

Sara went back to tying ribbon bows on the packets of cookies. "Yes. I've been a water baby since birth. Cathy and I have been friends forever. We went to elementary school together. With Heather. You haven't met her." Sara grinned. "Yet."

The cellophane crinkled when she slid it across the stainless steel counter. She grabbed another sheet full of cookies that needed packaging.

"Heather's mother bought this building years ago and turned it into a B&B," she told him. "I grew up playing hide and seek in that rambling house above us. Sliding down banisters, telling ghost stories that scared the wits out of Heather and Cathy, and knocking on doors of overnight guests for early morning wakeup calls they never ordered."

Sara watched Landon's shoulders shake as he chuckled.

"Sounds like the three of you were trouble," he said, grinning up at her.

"Oh, yeah. We were ornery, that's for sure. But what kid isn't, right?"

Growing up in Ocean City had been like a wonderful, never-ending dream. There was always something to do—crabbing in the bay, playing volleyball in the park, soaking up the sun on the beach, watching the sailboats come into the marina, shopping the outlets, surfing the waves, haunting the arcades. And during the warm months, a new batch of tourists hit town every week, not to mention the weekenders and day-trippers. There were always new people to meet, new friends to make.

"Summers were so much fun," she told

him. "I love this town. I've never had the desire to live anywhere else." The sigh that issued past her lips radiated her contentment. "There's just something about the ocean that, I don't know, just calls to me, you know?"

She was surprised to find he was still looking at her, studying her with a pensive gaze.

Finally, he offered a small nod. "Up until a couple years ago, I wouldn't have understood what you meant, but now I can say I do."

Couple of years? But hadn't he just said he'd seen the ocean for the first time a few weeks ago?

The words he'd spoken weren't nearly as intriguing as what he hadn't said. She wanted to ask him more questions, but for some reason she just couldn't bring herself to. The tone of his voice implied that—*whatever* he'd meant— it was both personal and profound.

They worked together for several minutes in companionable silence, Sara packaging cookies, Landon painstakingly smearing some sort of goop on the pipes and fittings before assembling them altogether.

"Listen," he said, "do you know where I might rent a room for a few nights?" he asked. "I'd like to have a chance to look around a little, but as I drove in from the north, I saw a lot of no vacancy signs."

"You don't have a reservation?"

"Nah." He shifted his position on the floor. "I've been winging it. It's October. I figured it's a little late in the year for the beach." Then he chuckled to himself. "Evidently, I was wrong."

"As long as the days are still warm, every beach-lover within a five hundred mile radius is trying to take advantage of the sun and sand."

He nodded. "I know that now. One night I had to drive nearly forty miles inland to find a place to sleep." He slid the solder and the torch closer to him. "You think there's a room here? At the B&B?"

Sara's shoulders rounded. "I'm sure The Loon is full. But wait..." She swiped her palms together a couple of times and then reached into her pocket to pull out her cell. "Let me text Heather," she said, thumbing out the message as she spoke. "Maybe there's been a last minute cancellation."

While waiting for Heather to respond, Sara explained, "There's a lot going on in town. I know there's a surf-fishing tournament this weekend. My next door neighbor is competing. I'm not sure what's happening at the convention center, but the parking lot was packed when I drove by. And people are already arriving for next week's car show. Have you seen the hot rods?"

"I did see a few souped up cars." Landon tugged at the bottom of his t-shirt. "I guess I'll be driving inland again—"

The phone vibrated against the metal counter and she picked it up. "I'm sorry. Heather says she's full. No cancellations. But she'll let me know if anything comes up." She tucked the phone away, then brightened as an idea came to her. "Listen, why don't you stay at my place?"

The friendly expression disappeared from Landon's face. "You're kidding me, right? Sara, you don't even know me. You can't invite a complete stranger to stay in your home. I could be a serial killer, for all you know."

Sara pressed her lips together to quell a smile. Finally, she asked, "You're not, are you? A serial killer, I mean."

He cocked one of his dark eyebrows. "This isn't funny, Sara. I'm serious. You don't know me. Even if you did, having me invade your space would be a major inconvenience. I can't do that to you. It just wouldn't be right, Sara. I don't mind driving inland to find a motel."

Every time he said her name, she felt a wonderful little thrill shoot through her.

"Why don't you let me decide what's an

inconvenience and what's not," she told him. "It'll be fine. You said it's only for a few nights. And besides that—" she shrugged "—I won't be there."

Confusion bit deeply into his forehead. "Where are you going?"

Now Sara laughed. "Would you relax? I'll be there. Just not *there*."

"That doesn't help me to understand."

"I'll stay downstairs. With my mom."

It was clear he needed more information.

"Landon, I don't know if you realize this, but land is a valuable commodity around here. People don't build out... they build up. I live in a duplex. Only the houses aren't side by side. They're stacked. I live upstairs. Mom lives downstairs."

"Sara, I can't push you out of your home," he said. "Even if it is for—"

"My, my," she murmured, picking up a cookie and moving toward him. "That frown is as deep as the Atlantic. Maybe this will make you smile." She broke the sugar cookie in half and bent over just enough so she could slip crisp confection between his lips; he took her offering without argument.

He chewed, and she could tell he enjoyed it. But just as the corners of his mouth began to curl upward and his eyes went all soft at the corners, he swallowed... and went completely still. His jaw muscles went slack enough that his lips parted. He stared up at her, his face turning pale enough to startle her.

"What is it?" she asked him. "You look like you've seen a ghost."

CHAPTER THREE

"LANDON COULDN'T SEEM to get out of there fast enough." Sara walked between Cathy and Heather, the wet sand flat and hard-packed at low-tide. "He didn't even finish his cookie. He asked me to go turn on the water so he could check the pipe splice for leaks, and by the time I returned from the utility room, he seemed in a frenzy, picking up the steel wool, that soldering thingie, and the other tools he'd used. I barely got to thank him before he bolted out the front door. He was completely shaken. I don't know what happened. After he was gone, I went to wash my hands so I could finish wrapping the cookies and saw half the cookie I gave him still sitting on the counter."

The three of them were enjoying their evening catch up. It was a ritual they rarely missed. During the long days of summer, they might spread out a blanket and soak up the last rays of the day while they talked. Or they might sit in the air-conditioned confines of The Sunshine Grill to chat over glasses of iced tea or lemonade. Sometimes they would walk down to Shenanigans for a beer, or to the Purple Moose for a glass of wine and some appetizers, or to Fisher's for some buttery caramel popcorn. There were so many places they could go along the boardwalk. Tonight, because the October evening was abnormally warm, they had decided to kick off their shoes, roll up their pant legs, and take a little stroll down by the edge of the ocean. Cooler temperatures were just over the horizon, so taking every advantage to get out on the beach was imperative.

After the heat of the day, the cool sand felt nice against Sara's bare feet and the rhythmic sound of the waves relaxed her.

"I mean, he went *stark white*," she stressed. "He didn't offer an explanation. And he looked so shaken. Almost frightened, really, as he'd stared at me. I... I..." Sara shook her head. "I tried to ask him about it, but there was a flurry of activity and then he was gone."

"Maybe he *had* seen a ghost." Cathy laughed. "Maybe Greg is haunting the shop and Landon saw his apparition. Ooo-ooooo-oo," she sang the macabre sound in several wavering high and low notes.

Heather came to a complete halt on the spot.

Caught off guard, Sara and Cathy took another step or two before they, too, stopped and turned around.

Chastisement tightened the muscles of Heather Phillip's pretty face and her fist rested firmly on her rounded hip. Heather was the quiet one of the group. So painfully shy as a child that she had ignited the protective instincts of both Sara and Cathy back when they had all first met in elementary school. Heather had spent the first twenty-eight years of her life in the shadow of her fun-loving, gregarious mother who had been a well-known and very well-loved personality in Ocean City. Heather suffered terribly when her mother had become a casualty of breast cancer nearly ten years ago, and that had only been the beginning of Heather's loss.

"Why would you say something like that?" Heather asked Cathy. "Don't plant that thought in Sara's head. Greg wouldn't haunt the sweet shop. He loved Sara. He wouldn't scare off a perfectly nice guy who is only trying to help her."

Cathy chuckled and waved her hands in the air as if she were brushing Heather's concerns away with the light, salty breeze. "I know that. I was joking. She knows I was only teasing her. Right, Sara?"

Sara stood with her feet rooted to the sand, the complicated mix of emotions that churned in her gut at the mention of Greg seemed to steal the words right out of her throat.

Heather moved toward her. "Sara, what is it? What's wrong? Cathy didn't mean it."

Already within arm's reach, Cathy placed a gentle hand on Sara's shoulder. "It wasn't Greg, honey. I shouldn't have said that. I was just teasing." Then she smirked. "It was probably the cookie. Did Landon gag? Was it dry? Did you add too much salt to the dough?"

Cathy's humorous ploy made Heather chuckle, but that didn't stop her from giving Cathy a little shove. "Shut up, already."

Then Cathy and Heather both sobered and focused on Sara.

"It's Greg," Sara said. "I just realized. I didn't think about him today. Not once. I spent almost the entire day with Landon Richards, and I didn't think about Greg. Not one time."

She tucked her bottom lip between her teeth for a second as she tried to figure out just how guilty she should feel. Sara waited for the tears of grief to burn her eyes, and she was surprised when they didn't come. That just thickened her shame even more.

"Don't be like this," Heather said. "Don't you feel guilty. It might not feel like it, but this is a good thing."

"It's a *very* good thing," Cathy agreed.

"How is it good?" Sara demanded.

Heather pressed her lips together for a moment, her long brown hair falling over her shoulder. "It means that... maybe you're healing."

Cathy nodded. "Maybe you're ready to stop wearing all that black."

Sara's spine went rigid. "I don't wear black." A surprising flash of anger speared through her.

"Not on the outside." Cathy's tone remained kid-glove soft. "But all three of us know that, ever since Greg's funeral, you've been living as if you had the word *widow* tattooed across your forehead. But, you know—" she offered a little smile and lifted one shoulder "—Heather's right. This is a good thing. Maybe you're ready to, you know, move on."

"But I don't want to move on!" The sharp words tumbled from her mouth before Sara could stop them. "Not if it means forgetting Greg. He was my husband. He was my *whole life*. For a lot of years. I don't want to forget him. I won't let—"

"Okay, okay. It's all right."

It was Heather's gentle voice that had Sara blinking her way out of the swirling vortex of anger and guilt. Sara stopped talking and looked out at the vast expanse of blue water. She took a deep, indrawn breath, held it for a moment, and then released it slowly.

"I'm sorry," she told her friends. "I was overwhelmed there for a second. I shouldn't have snapped at you like that. It's just..." She went quiet as tears blurred her vision.

"It's all right," Heather repeated. "We understand."

Evidently, Cathy felt a change of topic was in order because she asked Sara, "So Landon did a good job on the plumbing?"

"It was perfect," Sara told her. She swiped the back of her hand across her eyes as the three of them continued their walk on the beach. "And he was neat about it too. No mess when he was finished."

Cathy looked impressed. "That's a rare trait in a man."

Sara just smiled. Although she wished Cathy wasn't so hard-hearted when it came to the male of the species, Sara knew her friend had good reason. Her ex-husband had put her through the wringer during their drawn out divorce. When it was all over, Cathy had been left in financial ruin. The experience continued to color her general attitude about men.

"Oh," Sara said, "I almost forgot. He offered to come back tomorrow afternoon once the restaurant is closed and replace the main valve in the utility room. He said it should be replaced before it starts leaking, or fails altogether. He says it's all corroded."

"Yea!" Heather smiled broadly and clapped her hands. "That's great."

"I'd love a shut off valve by my kitchen sink at The Grill," Cathy said, excitement lacing her tone.

Heather's eyes went wide. "Oh, yes! I'd love one at the sink in my kitchenette upstairs, too."

"Wait. We can't do that to him," Sara said. "It wouldn't be fair. He's only in town for a few days."

"He's on vacation?" Cathy asked.

There was the slightest pause before Sara said, "Yeah, I think so."

She didn't elaborate because she wasn't completely sure why Landon was in town. His whole "need to see the ocean" story had sounded a little off. Not that wanting to visit the seashore was an odd thing, not by any stretch of the imagination, but as he'd explained to her how he'd come to drive over a thousand miles to see the Atlantic, she'd gotten the distinct impression—from the careful and even hesitant measure of his words—that the series of events still somehow confused *him* and that he hadn't quite figured it out for himself yet. Of course, she was doing nothing but speculating, but she'd been very intrigued when he'd said the New Jersey beaches hadn't felt "right." Of course, all of his uncertainty could be blamed on his being upset by having just sold the family business back in Kansas. Packing up and leaving your home, your work, your family, everything you knew and were comfortable with would be enough to discombobulate anyone.

"And he's staying at your place?" Heather asked.

Sara nodded. "I'll sleep downstairs at Mom's. I gave her a call, and she's happy to have me."

After Greg's accident, Sara had slept downstairs at her mother's house for weeks. Her sickly mom had welcomed her with open arms.

"Gosh," Cathy said softly, "I'd kill for a shut off valve."

Heather reached out and gave Cathy's forearm a quick squeeze. "Me too."

"I'm telling you, that would be asking too much of him," Sara repeated firmly. But the desolation in their voices and the pleading look in their eyes made her frown. "No. I mean it. We're getting a nozzle in the utility room and that's it. You can't ask for more of his time than that. It would be taking advantage of him."

Placing her palm flat against her chest, Heather said, "Well, I can't ask him, that's for sure. Rudeness isn't in my nature." Then she grinned. "But I'm sure Cathy wouldn't have a problem with it."

"Damn straight, I wouldn't." Cathy laughed.

Sara gave each of them a mock glare. "But you won't!"

"Okay." There was surrender in the two syllables Heather sang.

Cathy continued to laugh, her eyes twinkling as she looked at Heather. "It's a good thing Sara isn't the boss of me, huh?"

Before Sara could respond, a wave rushed onto the shore and splashed against their ankles and calves, pushing chilly water and sand up the legs of their pants and sending all three of them racing toward dry ground.

CHAPTER FOUR

IN 1933, A vicious hurricane traveled up the east coast, producing a storm surge that resulted in 100-year floods and caused ocean waves to tear at the shoreline, eroding the beach for hundreds of miles. The massive amount of water ate a fifty-foot crevasse through the southernmost tip of Ocean City and forever separated the town from the land that would become known as Assateague Island. The town administrators, who had long desired an inlet that would offer boaters and fishermen easy access between the bay and the ocean, seized on the prime opportunity nature had provided and built jetties to insure that the new waterway would remain open.

Landon had read about the creation of the inlet at the Life-Saving Station Museum. Although he'd arrived just before closing time, the kind woman who'd taken his entrance fee told him to take his time before once again burying her nose in the romance novel she'd been reading when he walked through the door. He'd trolled the cool confines of the small building located at the southern most end of the boardwalk, reading about the history of the town and the heroic deeds of the Surfmen of the US Life-Saving Service. He'd learned a lot about shipwrecks and rescues on Delmarva's coast.

It wasn't that shipwrecks intrigued him particularly, but getting lost in the details of such disasters as the Sallie Kaye, which broke up on the shore in 1882 during a blizzard, had been just what Landon needed to fend off the distress—no, *the shock*—he'd experienced when he'd been with Sara at her shop.

Now, he sat outside on a bench and watched a tall-masted sailboat pass through the channel. Small fishing boats struggled against the swift tidal currents in the narrow waterway. He'd had a friendly conversation with an elderly man who fished from the cement promenade that ran part of the length of the inlet.

He'd succeeded, for the past couple of hours at least, in sidestepping and outright avoiding thoughts about what had happened earlier. If it were possible, Landon would forget that the whole incident had occurred. Well, not *the whole* incident, of course, but most assuredly the final, freaky moments. If he could, he'd even go so far as to have the memory surgically removed; that's how much the weird, out-of-body experience disturbed him. But that was a ridiculous notion. Too bad thoughts and memories weren't susceptible to a surgeon's blade.

It had been only an instant, really. That one, explosive moment when Sara had fed him that cookie. The sweet, buttery taste had hit his tongue, he'd looked up into her beautiful green eyes, and—

His skin turned clammy despite the warm sunshine beaming down on him. He stood up suddenly, his gaze latching onto the windswept dunes on the island across the inlet. Then he turned and began to walk, his steps swift, as if he were hoping to escape whatever it was that was chasing him even though he knew that was impossible. The thoughts were in his head. A man couldn't run away from his own thoughts.

What he had experienced was strange.

Unexplainable. And being walloped by that overwhelming moment of déjà vu when he'd been with Sara hadn't been the beginning. Not by a long shot.

Months ago, the dreams had started. Vague, whispery images of azure blue skies, almost other-worldly, crystalline sunlight, and the waves. Always the waves. The rhythm of the ocean lapping at the shore seemed ever-present when he slept. Odd dreams for a land-locked farmer who had never set foot on a sandy beach in his life.

And then the other odd happenings began—when he'd been wide awake.

He'd tried to talk to his sister about what he was experiencing, but Cindy had laughed off his concerns. Then again, she laughed off most things. She was a busy wife and mother, trying to keep up with the housework and caring for her kids and heaps of laundry and cooking three full meals a day. Farming took a lot of physical energy and that required calories. Cindy had cooked for her husband and Landon and the three hired hands. Before they'd sold the farm, Cindy had worked as hard as, or harder than, any of them.

His brother-in-law hadn't been much help either. When Landon had approached him to talk about the dreams and his odd desire to visit the ocean, Henry had only continued to chew his toothpick and gaze out across the field of corn. After a few moments, Henry nodded and told Landon, "Don't you worry none. This, too, shall pass."

Later that same night, Landon couldn't help noticing that the beer had gone missing from the refrigerator, and the liquor cabinet had been locked, drum tight. At first, Landon had been annoyed by Henry's response. Then his irritation had flared into outright anger, but then he'd wondered what he would have done had he been in Henry's shoes and Henry had been the one complaining about the strange and unexplainable.

Hearing sounds that shouldn't exist, dreaming of far away places, being hit with crazy emotions, and thinking things he'd never thought about before. To a simple farm boy like Henry, these occurrences could be rationalized by one of just a few causes; biblical grace, demonic possession, imbibing an abundance of alcohol, or general insanity. Evidently, Henry had been most comfortable with the idea that Landon had developed a drinking problem, and he had solved it the best way he knew how—by removing access to the offending spirits.

So Landon had quickly learned to keep his experiences, his dreams, and his thoughts to himself, no matter how bizarre they became.

But in all the months that he'd been plagued, he'd never experienced a moment so profound, so utterly soul-shaking as when he'd been with Sara. More precisely, when he'd eaten that cookie. What the hell the cookie triggered in him was anyone's guess. It wasn't like he'd never enjoyed a sugar cookie before. Cindy had done plenty of baking at the farm. Was it that the cookie had been shaped like a pumpkin? Who the hell knew? It was October and Halloween wasn't far off, for cripes sake. Pumpkin-shaped cookies were everywhere this time of year.

All he did know for sure was that he'd been jolted to his very core.

He had clearly witnessed Sara's concern, but all he could think about was getting away from those walls that had begun closing in on him, fleeing from the chaos that churned both his thoughts and his emotions. Landon's need to burst out into the fresh air, into the openness of the outdoors had almost pushed him into behaving rudely. However, Sara must not have been too put off by his behavior because, before he'd left her bake shop, she'd jotted down her address and told him he could arrive any time after six.

Landon reached the end of the walkway

and turned to focus on the boats rocking on the choppy swells of the inlet. He reached up and smoothed his palm over his chest, the edges of the slip of paper Sara had given him evident beneath the fabric of his shirt pocket.

He glanced at his watch and nodded to himself. He was ready. He could arrive at her home and act like a normal human being. He could put what had happened behind him. He could banish it from his mind, and smile while carrying on a pleasant conversation just like any other sane individual.

He'd certainly had enough practice at it that was for damn sure.

CHAPTER FIVE

"YOU OKAY, MOM?" Sara tucked a lap blanket between her mother's hips and the plastic arms of the wheelchair.

Sara had arrived home in time to fix a light dinner of soup and salad. With her mom's condition, heavy meals just weren't something she was interested in and that was fine with Sara. Opening a tin of chicken with rice soup and dumping a bag of ready-made salad into a bowl made evening meals a breeze.

"I'm fine, hon. Stop worrying about me."

Sara just smiled and settled herself on a deckchair. Although she'd never say so, her mother was one of the biggest worries of her life.

This was one of Sara's and her mother's favorite times of the day. The sun shimmered like a liquid gold orb, slowly sinking toward the horizon. The backlit clouds glowed vibrant shades of lavender and yellow. It was a beautiful, breath-taking painting. And the best thing about it was, there would be a brand new one for everyone's enjoyment at this same time tomorrow.

The sound of a truck pulling up to the curb had Sara grinning. She was so glad that Landon hadn't missed the sunset.

"He's here," she whispered to her mom, hopping up from her seat.

Landon got out of his truck and lifted his hand in greeting. Judging from the plastic bag he carried, Sara surmised that he'd visited one of the grocery stores.

"I've got eyes," her mother quipped. "Why didn't you tell me he was such a broad-shouldered, good-looking guy?"

"Mom. Stop. He'll hear you." Why was it that, with a single observation, parents could make you feel all of thirteen again?

Her mother only chuckled.

Landon stepped up onto the deck. "Hi."

"Hey there," Sara greeted him. "You made it in time for the sunset."

He looked out over the water, and she took the opportunity to study his features. His cheekbones were high and his brow bone was strong. She wondered if he might have some Native Americans climbing around on a limb or two in his family tree.

Her mother shifted in her wheelchair, drawing Sara's attention. Her mom's arched eyebrows made Sara flush with embarrassment at having been caught staring.

"And it's a gorgeous one too," Landon said.

Sara took a step closer to him. "Landon, I told my mom that you'd be staying for a few days. I'd like for you to meet her," Sara said. "Mom, this is Landon Richards. He came to my rescue today at the shop. If he hadn't fixed that pipe, I don't know what we'd have done. Landon, this is my mom, Geneva Hartford."

Landon walked the length of the deck and gingerly shook the woman's hand. "Mrs. Hartford."

Geneva smiled up at him, her eyes twinkling with teasing. "I'm not made of glass, Landon. I won't break. I promise. And please call me Geneva. I haven't been Mrs. Hartford for a very long time."

The two of them exchanged pleasantries for a few moments, Geneva thanking him for helping her daughter with her water fountain disaster, and Landon assuring her he'd been happy to do it.

"Have you had dinner?" Sara asked him. "I have some soup and a salad inside, if you're hungry."

Landon lifted the grocery bag he carried. "Thanks, but I bought myself a frozen pizza. I thought that would be easy enough. Bought a few other items too. Can of coffee and a pint of cream. Bar of soap, that kind of thing."

"Sara, take your young man upstairs and show him around."

Tipping her head sideways, Sara silently scolded her mother. Then she sighed. Geneva grinned, obviously enjoying her daughter's discomfort.

Sara sobered. "Do you want me to wheel you in?"

"You know very well I can get myself inside. I'm going to sit here a while longer and enjoy the sky. Now, go." Geneva looked at Landon. "You have a good night. It was a pleasure meeting you."

"Likewise," Landon told her.

"The stairs to my place are around the side." Sara pointed.

To an out-of-towner, the configuration of the building might have looked odd. The front of the house faced the water and the side of the house faced the street. Nearly everyone in the area who lived on water-front property installed as many windows and sliding doors as they could in order to take full advantage of the water view. The wide, sturdy staircase that offered access to Sara's place was close to where Landon had parked his truck.

Sara led the way. "I should have told you that I have plenty of coffee and other staples. You're welcome to anything I've got up here. Shampoo, toothpaste, whatever." She stuck the key in the lock and the bolt unlatched with a loud click. She grinned over her shoulder. "I'm taking my toothbrush with me, though. I hope you brought your own."

Landon chuckled. "I'm good, thanks. It's in my bag in the truck. I'll bring my stuff up a little later. You're sure this isn't an imposition, Sara?"

"Absolutely positive." She pushed open the door and automatically reached for the switch that turned on the living room lamps. "We rent my place once in a while. Especially during the summer months. We have some regulars who come for long weekends, and one or two who stay a full week at a time. The rental income helps to supplement Mom's disability which is pretty paltry, to tell you the truth." Sara shook her head, her mouth flattening.

His dark eyes widened just a bit. "If your mother is in need of money, you have to let me pay you for—"

"No." She spoke the tiny word firmly and reached out to him. She became instantly and acutely aware of the heat emanating from his skin when she slid her fingers over the firm muscles of his forearm. The need to moisten her lips was strong, and her throat felt dry when she swallowed. She pulled back and slowly lowered her hand to her side.

"There's no need to rehash this again, Landon," she told him, hoping her tone covered the sudden shakiness she felt in the pit of her gut. "You're helping me. And my friends. Let us give you something in return. It's called bartering, and it's a perfectly good business practice."

"Okay, okay," he said. He moved further into the house toward the kitchen table.

The main living area of her home was wide open and encompassed the living room, kitchen and dining area. The cathedral ceiling gave the space an airy feel and made it seem bigger than it actually was. The dining area boasted a wide, eastern-facing picture window that let in the morning sunlight, and the eight foot sliding door off the living room offered a wide, unobstructed view of the bay to the west.

Now that the sun had dipped below the horizon, fat threads of golden light wove through the purplish twilight.

"I won't bring it up again," Landon promised. He set his grocery bag on the table and began unpacking its contents.

The soft denim of his faded jeans hugged his butt and thighs. The sight had Sara feeling suddenly too warm and she tucked her bottom lip between her teeth. Ogling this man was the last thing she should be doing, so she turned and made a beeline for the kitchen.

"Listen, I hope you don't mind my asking, but..."

Landon hesitated so long, Sara turned to look at him.

"I won't mind. Ask away."

"What happened to your mom?" He stopped unpacking, but the plastic bag crinkled when he turned toward her. "I mean, why is she... you know..." He shook his head and murmured, "I'm sorry. No matter how I try to say it, it's going to sound rude. I shouldn't have brought it up. But...it's just that she looks awfully young to be, well..."

"Confined to a wheelchair?" Sara finished for him.

She opened the oven and pulled out the cookie sheets she had stored there and then snapped on the oven. "What temperature do you need? For the pizza?"

"Oh, thanks." Landon grabbed the box and turned it over. "Four hundred degrees."

"It won't take long to pre-heat." She moved to the sink and began putting away the dishes she'd washed before leaving for the shop that morning. "Mom's been diagnosed with spinal stenosis. It's a narrowing of the channel within the spinal column and it presses on the nerves. She's in a good bit of pain almost every day. Thankfully, she hasn't lost her ability to walk, and on good days she can get around pretty well. Today, well..." She shook her head slowly. "It isn't a good day."

She moved to the coffee maker, plunked in a filter, and then filled the pot with water as she talked. "The problem was caused by a fall down a flight of concrete steps. I must have been about nine or ten at the time. We've been to several different doctors and all of them tell us that surgery might help, or that it might end up making matters worse. They can't say for sure, and no one will offer any guarantees." She turned, leaned her hip against the counter and crossed her arms. "Mom's too afraid to have surgery, so we're taking it one day at a time."

Landon closed the refrigerator door after storing away the cream he'd bought. "That's an awful thing to have to deal with. But I do know what you mean by taking things one day at a time."

She waited, certain he meant to elaborate, but he didn't. So she told him, "Luckily, Mom has lots of friends. They've sort of made up a loose schedule so that she has a visitor most days. I'm really grateful because, otherwise, I'd be worried sick while I was at the shop and running around town making my deliveries."

"Deliveries?"

"I bake desserts for several restaurants in town. We're coming up on the end of the tourist season, so things will be slacking off soon. But a few businesses stay open year round. Like Cathy does." A sudden thought had her pushing herself away from the counter. "I'd better put fresh sheets on the guest bed."

"Oh, wait," he said, following after her out of the kitchen and down the hall, "I can do that, Sara."

The way he said her name, all soft and sonorous, sent a delicious thrill shooting up the full length of her spine, and her skin erupted in gooseflesh. She was so glad she had her back to him.

"I don't mind," she told him in a rush. She opened the linen closet and pulled a set of neatly folded, yellow sheets off the shelf as well as fresh bath towels, a hand towel, and a washcloth. "Besides, I know where everything is."

She set the linens on the dresser and then pulled the comforter and pillows off the queen size bed. "Do you know the population of Ocean City can run as high as three hundred and fifty thousand during the summer months?" She balled up the sheets she removed from the bed and reached for the clean ones. "In the dead of winter, there are under eight thousand full-time residents."

Why she chose this moment to offer up that random factoid was anyone's guess.

"Wow, that's a huge disparity."

Sara glanced at Landon, who stood awkwardly in the doorway with his hands in his pockets.

"Listen," he said, "do you mind if I at least give you a hand? I don't want you thinking I'm some sort of helpless idiot."

Blinking up at him, she felt her face go hot. "I don't think that." She tucked a corner of the fitted sheet into place, grateful for a task to focus all her efforts on long enough to gather her wits. The man made her thoughts go haywire. Then she bent down and snatched a pillow from where it had landed on top of the comforter. "Here you go." She tossed the pillow at him and it bounced off his chest.

"Oh, my gosh. I'm sorry." But her apology got lost in her sudden bout of nervous laughter.

"Hey, I wasn't ready."

"Sorry," she murmured, and then she pressed her lips together tightly in an attempt to squash the humor that threatened to bubble up again. "You always have to be ready when you're around me. You never know what I might do next."

"Mm-hmm." He picked up the pillow. "I can see that."

A renewed flush heated her face. What was *wrong* with her? If she didn't know better, she'd say she was flirting with this man. *Flirting?* The mere idea had her swallowing nervously.

No way. She was just putting him at ease. That was all she was doing.

He put fresh cases on the pillows and then moved to help her smooth out the top sheet.

Her gaze zeroed in on his hand and how he ran the flat of his palm across the expanse of the soft, Egyptian cotton. She chewed on her bottom lip at the same time as her pulse began thudding between her thighs.

What on earth was going on with her?

"So do you keep your shop open?"

His quiet question took her off guard. She

straightened, her hands falling to her sides, and looked at him across the bed.

"Keep my shop open?" she asked. She heard the far-away quality of her own voice. The truth was that it hadn't been his question that startled her; it had been the physical reactions she was having to him. Feeling attraction after such a long time... It was odd. And kind of scary.

"Off-season," he explained. And when she still didn't answer, he offered, "Through the winter?"

His expression told her he wanted to ask her if she was okay, that he was confused by her inability to keep up with their simple conversation.

"I, uh, I close the front of the shop after Thanksgiving because there's little foot traffic on the boardwalk. But I bake all year long." She said the words quickly. "For Cathy's grill. For Heather's guests. For a few restaurants that stay open. And I've recently started a small mail-order business. I've mailed cookies all over the US. You saved a huge batch of those today."

"Ah, so you're an entrepreneur. That's great."

Just as they'd tucked the comforter back into place and put the pillows on the bed, the buzzer on the oven sounded.

"Oh, we should put your pizza in to bake." Sara couldn't seem to leave the bedroom fast enough. She went down the hall, into the kitchen, and picked up the box that had been sitting on the counter.

"Sara," he said.

Both his hands slid overtop of hers, stilling their nervous motion.

"Please, stop. I can do that for myself."

She looked up into his handsome face, into those dark, serious eyes studying her.

"Of course," she murmured. "I'm sure you can."

Skimming her tongue across her lips, she slid her hands from beneath his and left him holding the box. "I should get out of here and let you get on with... things." She took a couple of backward steps, inhaling deeply. "There's a stacked washer and dryer in the laundry closet in the hallway. Detergent is on the shelf. You can't miss it. The dishes are in the cabinet there. The pantry's pretty full." She pointed. "Use whatever you need. I mean it. Make yourself at home."

"Thanks," he told her. "You sure you don't want some pizza?"

"I'm sure." She moved closer to the door. "Keys to the place are on the table by the door.

Feel free to open the windows. Or switch on the heat if you need to. Your bedroom has a ceiling fan. There's a switch on the wall. Oh, as soon as you get up, just turn on the coffee maker. You'll have a fresh pot in less than ten minutes. And there's a baking sheet for your pizza right on top of the stove there." Again she pointed.

He didn't turn to look in the direction she indicated, he just nodded and stood there holding the pizza still in its box.

Sara pulled open the front door. "You could come to The Grill for breakfast, if you like. I leave for work early, so I'll see you over there. Whenever you get there is fine. You can sleep in if you want to." God, she'd never babbled this much in her entire life.

Again, he nodded and smiled.

"Good night," she said.

"Good night."

When she closed the door, he was still standing there in the kitchen. It took her a second or two to realize he was looking at her through the glass. She lifted her hand and then turned away.

The sky had turned a deep indigo and stars shined against the darkness.

What the heck? She wanted to cringe with embarrassment. Anyone eavesdropping on that mostly one-sided conversation would think she had just met a brand new species and was trying like hell to make a good impression. There at the end, her mouth had been running as fast as a broken faucet.

She hurried down the stairs, rounded the corner of the building and let herself into her mom's front door. Soft light lit the empty living room, and the stillness in the air told her that her mother must have headed to her bedroom. Sara knocked before she opened the door.

"Hey. Just wanted to check on you and say good night." Sara smiled and moved to the bed to give her mother a kiss. The light, familiar scent of her mom's moisturizing cream wafted up to meet her.

"Did you get your young man all settled?"

"Mom, he's not my young man," Sara admonished. "You need to stop that. He's just a guy. A guy who's helping us with the plumbing over at the Loon. That's all."

"Okay. All right. I'll stop." Her mother smiled softly. "But it's been a long time since I've seen you roll your eyes at me like that."

Sara just shook her head, her shoulders rounding. "I just made a complete fool of myself up there just now. I treated the man like he was an imbecile. I got the coffee maker ready for in the morning. I turned on the oven for his pizza. I made his bed. I'm afraid I would have cooked his dinner and fed it to him if he hadn't stopped me." She sighed. "And I talked, non-stop."

"Oh, don't worry so much. I'm sure he was happy to have the company." Then she tilted her head a bit. "You would never admit this yourself, Sara, so I'm going to go ahead and say it. It's nice to have a man around."

"He's not staying long," Sara felt the need to emphasize, for her mom *and* herself.

Geneva nodded and shifted on the mattress, a grimace shadowing her lovely face.

"You okay?" Sara asked. "Do you need anything?"

"I'm good, honey. I'm going to watch my sit-coms and then I'm going to sleep." She reached for her glass of water and took a sip. "I've got a pain pill here for later, if I need it."

"Okay. You call me if you need anything, you hear?"

They exchanged good-nights, and then Sara closed her mom's door and went to her room. She pulled off her top and tossed it onto the nearby chair and her phone trilled with a text message alert.

Heather: How's your mom?
Sara: Well enough to put herself to bed.
Heather: Good! Did Landon get settled?
Sara: Sure did.

Heather: I decided you're right. We can't impose on him any more than we already have. Did you warn him about Cathy?
Sara: No. Forgot. But I will first thing tomorrow.
Heather: He's a cute one, huh?

Sara just stared at the screen, uncertain of how she should respond. She wanted to spill her guts, tell Heather about how she'd fallen all over herself upstairs trying to help him, and how she'd prattled on incessantly, like an inexperienced teenager. Not to mention that she'd felt heat spark to life in parts of her that hadn't even been lukewarm since Greg had passed away.

Greg. She closed her eyes and heaved a sigh as a dark shadow hovered over her, heavy as wet wool. She flopped down on her mattress and stared up at the ceiling.

Once again, Greg hadn't entered her thoughts the entire time she'd been upstairs with Landon, talking, laughing, *flirting.*

"I wasn't flirting." Sara whispered the words aloud, and even as she uttered them, she knew she was lying.

God, she was lonely. Maybe Heather and Cathy were right. Maybe it was time to move on. But even as the words echoed through her head, the guilt seemed to press in on her. It bothered her that her friends thought she lived with a "widow" mentality. It's not that she purposefully pushed men away. It was just...

Again she sighed. Why was moving forward so damned hard?

The phone she clutched against her belly trilled and she lifted it to look at the screen.

Heather: ???
Sara: Yes. He's cute. Correction. He's hot!
Heather: Clear out the cobwebs, honey. You just might get lucky. ;)
Sara: LOL He's only in town a few days.
Heather: You can get a whole lotta lucky in a few days. Sweet dreams!

Sara just laughed as she set the phone on her nightstand. Heather and Cathy both were absolutely crazy, and thank goodness for that.

Faint sounds of water running came from her unit upstairs. Landon must have decided to take a shower while his dinner was in the oven.

She closed her eyes, imagining herself in the steamy bathroom, inhaling the scent of masculine soap, gliding her fingers over wet, slick skin. There it was again, that heady pulsing at the apex of her thighs, that itch that needed scratching.

Her belly felt firm and flat as she slid her palm downward. What would it feel like to have his hands on her body? She stopped when her fingertips dipped beneath the waistband of her pants.

She groaned, rolled off the mattress and onto her feet. She had to stop this. It was nuts. She'd just met Landon Richards. He was a complete stranger. Then her mom's words whispered through her head.

It's nice to have a man around.

That was true. Today had proven it. She'd enjoyed being with him, stranger or not.

So what if he'd only be in town for a few days? Like Heather said, a person could get a whole lot of "lucky" in a few days. Besides, Sara didn't need a whole lot. It would only take a little bit of lucky to satiate her itch.

The nonsensical thought made Sara's shoulders shake with laughter as she snatched up her robe and headed toward the hallway bathroom for a shower of her own.

CHAPTER SIX

"COME ON IN," Sara called when she heard the soft rap on the back door of her shop, knowing it had to be Landon. Heather wouldn't have bothered knocking, and Cathy had gone home hours ago. It was too late for deliveries.

"Hey," he greeted. "I'm finished with the nozzle in the utility room and the water's back on. Just wanted to let you know."

"Thanks. It's almost dark. You missed the sunset." She offered him a quick glance and then focused her attention on the cupcake she was decorating.

"Yeah, one of the couplings didn't want to, you know, couple." He chuckled. "But I finally wrangled the thing under control."

"You must be starving. How about I buy you dinner?"

She sensed rather than saw him frown.

"You don't have to do that."

"I know I don't," she told him. "But I want to. I'm sorry Cathy talked you into more plumbing work."

"Aw, it's nothing, really. I can install cut-off valves at all the sinks that don't have one. One each day, six sinks in the house. If I don't run into any complication, I'll be out of your hair in a week. If you don't mind me staying at your place, that is."

"Nope, don't mind a bit." She piped the last dollop of black icing near the center. "There! Done. One last cupcake and I'll be finished. Then we can go find you something to eat."

Landon looked at the trays of cupcakes, smiling at her handiwork. "Those are so neat. They look just like little wiry-haired puppy faces. Some kid is going to be very happy."

Sara picked up the final, bare cupcake in one hand and the bag of white icing in the other. Then she began making squiggles.

"Believe it or not," she told him, "these are for an adult party. A restaurant owner here in town is throwing a birthday party for his schnauzer tomorrow afternoon. He does it every year. You'll read about the party in the Dispatch later this week." She dropped her voice to a whisper. "Even the mayor will be there."

Landon laughed, and the deep rumble of it forced Sara to stop her work and look over at him. His brown eyes crinkled at the corners, and she felt a nervous twitter tighten in her belly. The man sure was easy to look at.

"Are you invited?" he asked.

"Oh, no." She shook her head. "I don't travel in those circles."

Sara worked in silence for a few seconds, feeling his gaze on her as she twisted the cupcake one way, then another, in order to get the entire top decorated.

"You're very talented."

"It's all in the wrist." To prove her point, she flicked perfect curlicues across the cake surface.

His tone lowered as he said, "I can see that."

She barreled ahead. "Landon, I can do things with buttercream frosting that would blow your mind."

"I have no doubt."

A couple of things happened simultaneously; she realized there had been a couple of heartbeats of swollen silence before he responded, and she replayed the words she'd just spoken in her head. She blanched and her hands went still. Then her lips parted, but no words came out. She set down the bag of icing and the cupcake on the stainless steel counter and tried to smile, but failed.

She blinked and gazed into his eyes, saw the desire smoldering there.

"That came out sounding much more, um..." She searched the air for a proper word, licking her lips and drawing her brows together. "Eh, ah, *inappropriate* than I intended."

One corner of his mouth tipped upward. "I think it sounded perfectly appropriate, Sara."

The air left her lungs at the sound of her name. How did he do that? Say her name so softly, yet make it sound so rich, and resonant, and full of emotion?

The oddest feeling churned in her chest, a heated giddiness that made it difficult for her to draw breath. Her arms felt shaky, and she set the cupcake on the counter so she could clutch the cold, rounded metal edging. She needed the support, and besides that she hoped to hide the tremble of her hands.

He was attracted to her. *Wanted* her. She'd have had to be stone-cold unconscious not to recognize it.

Before meeting Landon, she hadn't thought about touching or being touched in a sexual way for a long, *long* time. She'd have thought desire was something she'd completely forgotten how to feel. But the human body was an amazing machine. Adrenalin surged and hormones coursed as a hot, greedy need thudded through her. Even as she stood at the island with at least three feet of space between them, she could feel herself being drawn to him like opposite poles of a magnet. The attraction was powerful. Too strong to be denied.

How they came together was anyone's guess. Had she moved toward him, he toward her? Or had they converged simultaneously? Sara couldn't be sure.

When she lifted her hands to place them on his chest, she noticed a smear of frosting on the side of her index finger, and she made to pull away so she could wipe her hand on her apron. But Landon captured her wrist and guided her finger to his lips. He slowly ran his tongue along her skin, the wet heat forced her breath to snag in her throat. Then he closed his lips around the pad of her finger and sucked gently.

"Mmmmm." The low, husky sound reverberated from deep in his chest. "Delicious."

"Come on now," she whispered, sensual

teasing in the words as she nuzzled his chin with the tip of her nose and then a light touch of her lips, "don't you think you should share?"

His arms wrapped around her and he kissed her languidly, once, twice, three times, and then he covered her mouth with his, delving his tongue into the soft and willing recesses.

She closed her eyes and reveled in the luscious taste of sugar and butter and vanilla and *him*. Without thought, she leaned into him, drawing back her shoulders just a little and pressing her breasts into his chest. Oh, to be naked and feel the heat of his bare skin against hers; that would be wonderful. The desire urging her on was all-consuming; she didn't have time to think about her actions, or to feel embarrassed by her bold behavior. She wanted to taste more of his kisses, she yearned to feel his hands on her body, she hungered for more... so much more.

Reaching around behind her, she tugged at the bow of her apron. All it took was a small arch of her spine and the fabric slid to floor. She nudged it aside with her foot.

Landon's hands splayed across her back and she was sure he must feel the thundering of her heart beneath her ribs. The kisses he rained on her neck stirred a fever in her. His thick, tawny hair felt like silk when she combed her fingers through it.

He picked her up and turned, perching her bottom on the edge of the metal counter. The filmy fabric of her full-skirted sundress draped across and between her legs and rode high on her thighs. Instinct had her wrapping her legs around him, and she pulled him up tight against her. The hard length of him bulged beneath the fabric of his jeans, the delicious stiffness snuggling against her throbbing need.

When he looked at her, his dark eyes were dazed.

"My god, Sara, what are we doing?"

The thrilling euphoria had her feeling a little dizzy. She grinned wickedly. "It's pretty obvious, isn't it?"

He swallowed, licked his lips, hungrily searched her gaze. All she could think about was tasting his kiss, his tongue, his skin.

"But we just met yesterday. We barely know each other." His voice was raspy with passion. "We need to talk. I have things I should tell you. Things you need to know…"

She silenced him with a long, luscious kiss, and when she broke it off, they were both breathing hard.

"And I'm sure there are things I should tell you," she panted against his wet mouth.

"Things like assuring you that I'm not this kind of woman." She closed her eyes when he kissed her temple. "Usually." She dragged air into her lungs. "I don't fall into bed easily."

They kissed again. And again.

"Things like this don't happen to me," she told him.

His skin felt feverish to the touch when she skimmed her fingertips down his cheek, along his jaw, and over the curves of his ears. She kissed his forehead and then kissed his mouth.

Sara felt so turned on, she was uncertain that she could hold off her orgasm until they actually did anything that could truly be called sex.

Dipping his chin, he broke off the kiss, and quickly gazed into her eyes.

"I could say the same thing, Sara." The words came out sounding like a groan. "But what if this is wrong? What if this is something we'll regret?"

She heard his questions and knew he was offering her a chance to stop. But even as he said the words, he continued to smooth his hands over her arms and shoulders, and his ravenous gaze never stopped roving over her face.

"If this is a mistake," she said, "it's one I want to make. No regrets, Landon. I promise."

That seemed to be all the permission he needed. The onslaught of his kisses strummed and plucked the strings of her emotions—and the music he created in her was erotic and melodious, like the bluesy strains of slow jazz. He slipped his hands beneath her, scooped her up by cupping her butt in his palms.

He held her against him low enough that she could start working at the buckle of his belt.

"The chair," she ordered him. "*The chair*."

He'd only taken two steps when she said, "Wait. The door. *The door*."

He carried her to the back door of the shop and she threw the bolt.

By the time they reached the chair that sat in front of a small desk in the corner of the kitchen, she'd unbuckled his belt and unfastened his jeans. He set her on her feet long enough for her to slide his trousers down over his hips. A small push on his shoulder propelled him into the chair. Sara wiggled out of her panties and straddled him, not yet sitting but keeping her knees straight. She bent at the waist, skimmed her hands over his muscular shoulders while she planted tiny kisses on his mouth.

A small moan erupted from the back of his throat, and the sound of it churned up a giddy feeling in her. She loved that she could elicit such a reaction in him.

Landon reached out, gliding his fingertips up the sides of her torso and stopping at the perfect spot that allowed him to draw firm circles around her budded nipples with his thumbs. Now it was her turn to gasp breathily, and when she dragged her eyelids open, she saw that his sexy mouth was curled into a small, luscious smile.

If he could make her feel this good while she was still fully dressed—or nearly so, anyway—how delicious would it be if they were totally nude?

The question whispered through her head, but she dismissed it almost before it had formed. She wanted *this*. Right here. Right now.

He chose that moment to skitter one hand beneath the hem of her dress, slowly gliding his fingers along the inside of her thigh. She was hot and wet and ready for him.

And he was ready for her. In one smooth motion, she gently grasped him, curled her hips, and lowered herself onto his lap.

Their kisses were deep and deliberate as she rocked her hips back and forth, back and forth, against him, slowly at first, and then faster. And faster. His hands had settled around her waist, hers cradled his head.

They convulsed together, their chests heaving as if they had just sprinted the full length of the boardwalk.

"That was wonderful," she whispered. *"Wonderful."*

Slowly, she became aware that something was... off. She frowned as she looked around her. Although they'd begun their lovemaking next to the desk she used to jot down recipes and pay bills, they'd ended the session at least eight feet away by the back door of the shop. The wheels on the chair hadn't offered a single squeak of warning that they'd been in motion. Then again, maybe they had and Sara simply hadn't heard it.

"How did we get all the way over here?" she asked, offering him a salacious grin.

"I don't know." His dark eyes twinkled with humor. "But I wouldn't be lying if I said that was the best ride of my life."

Sara laughed as she hugged him to her.

CHAPTER SEVEN

SARA, HEATHER, AND Cathy sat at a table on the outside deck at Fager's Island where they were enjoying delicious Orange Crushes, a popular cocktail served at the restaurant. The sun hung low in the sky, gilding the stringy lines of clouds with a coppery gold hue. Strains of the live stage act floated out of the building where a local singer crooned his rendition of Georgia, sounding a whole lot like Ray Charles.

Four days had passed since Sara and Landon had locked themselves inside her shop and engaged in delectable, soul-satisfying sex on her desk chair. *On her desk chair*. The idea made her press her lips together to stifle the grin that threatened to take over her mouth even now. They'd spent every day, or at least a good portion of them, together. Sara woke up each morning with a happy anticipation that she hadn't felt in a very long time.

"So," Cathy said, leaning toward Sara, "what's going on between you and Landon?"

Sara shifted her gaze to watch Landon at the bar where he was waiting for the beer he'd ordered. He smiled at her, and she couldn't help but smile back.

"Going on?" she said in response to Cathy's question. She inserted as much innocence as she thought she could get away with. These women knew her too well for her to tell them an outright lie.

"Oh, please." Cathy sucked on her straw.

"Give it up," Heather demanded. "We want to know everything."

Sara looked from one to the other. "What makes you think there's anything going on?"

She knew deflecting would only last so long. They'd been friends for too many years for them to allow her to get away with it.

"I'll tell you what makes us think something is going on." Cathy set her glass on the table. "Reason number one, he installed a cut-off valve at your sink *first*."

Sara waved off Cathy's words. "That's just

because I took him to the hardware store to begin with. Plus..." She smirked. "I keep him supplied with fresh-baked cookies."

"I fix him breakfast every morning," Cathy pointed out, saying it in a tone that clearly conveyed she was confused about why Landon would find her pancakes and fluffy eggs second-rate.

"Reason number two," Heather said, "he's not getting much plumbing done because the two of you are always off gallivanting to who knows where."

"Wait a minute." Sara leaned back and crossed her arms under her breasts. "He's not your hired handyman. He doesn't have to work every single day. So what if he's a little behind schedule? He has limited working hours. And if he wants to ride with me to deliver desserts, it should be no concern of yours. He'll install your shut-off valves soon enough. Besides, the man's on vacation. I'm only trying to show him the sights."

They both looked dubious.

Heather stirred her drink. "Reason number three. You two have been grinning like deliriously happy monkeys for days."

"We have not," Sara objected. "And I'm insulted that you'd compare us to wild animals."

But the memory of their lusty love-making made Sara realize Heather's description might not have been too far off the mark.

"Reason number four," Cathy said, "you invited Landon to a Girl's Night."

This accusation was a little harder to defend. There was almost nothing more sacred than Girl's Night Out. The three of them had enjoyed dinner out together at least once a month, and nothing had ever intruded on their habit—not business, not boyfriends, not husbands, nothing.

"Landon doesn't know anyone in town," Sara began, but she knew that wasn't going to fly even before the words left her mouth. He was a grown man, fully capable of occupying his free time all on his own. So she took another tack. "Every tourist should experience a sunset at Fager's Island at least once."

Almost immediately, both Heather and Cathy acquiesced with a silent nod.

"Everything is fine," Sara assured them. "He and I are just friends." She couldn't go any further than that without blatantly lying to them.

She lifted her gaze toward the bar and watched Landon as he accepted his beer and turned to walk toward them. The look he gave her ignited something deep in her belly.

"Reason number five," Heather said, her voice low, "friends don't look at each other like that."

Sara blinked and her mouth went dry. "Like what?"

Cathy gasped. "Oh, my God. You're sleeping with him."

"I am not sleeping with him," Sara insisted. "I'm sleeping at Mom's. You know that."

Heather's left eye narrowed just a fraction. "But you are having sex with him."

It wasn't a question. The jig was up, and Sara knew it.

"Keep your voice down," she whispered. "Everyone on the deck will hear you. Okay, okay. We had sex. It was only once. Just once. Now shut up about it. He's coming."

Cathy's spine straightened. "But we need more—"

Sara shot Cathy a look that sheared off the rest of her friend's sentence.

Landon slid onto the bench beside Sara. "That singer is great. He's done Sinatra, Ray Charles, Tom Jones, Elvis. I'm really enjoying the music."

Picking up her drink, Sara offered Landon a bright smile, knowing full well it was forced. And just as she feared, he didn't miss the fact that Heather and Cathy both looked like they were about to implode. There was a question in his gaze when he focused on her.

Sara stood up, still clutching her Orange Crush. "It's almost time."

"For what?" Landon asked.

"You two stay," Sara ordered Cathy and Heather. "Try to get hold of yourselves. Landon, let's walk out to the gazebo to watch the sunset. Bring your beer."

He seemed all too eager to escape what could quickly become an awkward moment.

Sara and Landon had barely taken a couple of steps before Heather and Cathy burst out laughing.

"What's going on?" he asked Sara.

"That seems to be the million dollar question of the evening," she murmured. She led him down the wooden pier that led to a covered gazebo built out over the bay waters.

"They were looking at me like I was a slab of prime rib on a hot dinner plate," he said.

Prime rib. Such an apt description, Sara mused.

Just as they stepped up to the railing, he said, "Damn, Sara. Did you tell them? About you and me, I mean?"

"I didn't have to tell them. They guessed. I can't keep anything from them." Sara wanted to be annoyed with Heather and Cathy. She wanted to be angry about their nosiness. But she couldn't muster up that kind of emotion when it came to her friends.

She sighed and tried to explain. "Then again, they can't keep anything from me, either."

At that moment, the 1812 Overture began to herald the sunset. After hearing the first strains of Tchaikovsky's masterpiece, Landon raised his brows and smiled in pleasant surprise, then he turned to watch the sun slide lower and lower on the horizon in tandem to the music. The sky glowed with radiant shades of yellow, red, and purple, and Landon reached down and curled his fingers around Sara's hand. She inched closer until the full lengths of their arms were touching. Just as the sun disappeared, the sound of cannon fire exploded through the night. The crowd behind them cheered and clapped their approval.

Landon bent over and rested his elbows on the banister, keeping hold of her hand as he did.

"Well, that sure was something to see," he said. His dark eyes took in every aspect of her face, and he slowly lifted her hand and planted a warm kiss on the backs of her fingers. "Thanks for inviting me tonight."

"I'm happy you're here." Even as the words

were slipping off her tongue, she knew she'd never uttered a truer statement. She was happy. Happy that she was with Landon. Happy that he held her hand. Happy that he seemed so pleased to be with her.

"Now," he said, softly, "about your friends. Do I need to worry? I mean, are they going to give me a hard time about, you know..." He pointed at her, then at himself. "You and me."

"Oh, who knows what's going on in their heads? But you won't be their target," she told him. "I'm the one with a bull's eye on her chest. But I don't mind." She chuckled as she shrugged. "'Cause I would be doing the same to them. In fact, it may sound crazy, but teasing the hell out of each other is how we prove our love."

Landon laughed, then he did the unexpected—he hugged her. Instantly, Sara feared she would tense up, graceless and stiff, against him because she knew her friends must be watching, but that wasn't what happened at all. No, she melted into him as if it were second nature and thought, *Let them look.*

CHAPTER EIGHT

I<small>T WAS NEARLY</small> midnight when the first group text arrived.

> Heather: Can't sleep. Hope I didn't wake you. Been laying here for an hour wondering.
> Cathy: About what? U okay?
> Sara: Yeah, what Cathy asked. You okay?
> Heather: Fine. Just restless. Thinking. Making love/having sex. What's the difference? Opinions, pls.
> Cathy: Oh, come on. What r u? 12?
> Sara: lol You need the birds and bees talk?
> Heather: I'm serious. As long as you get your rocks off, they're the same, right?

No new texts posted for a long, drawn out moment. Both Sara and Cathy had been married at one time, and although Cathy's marriage hadn't ended well—oh, hell, it had ended horribly—both of the women had loved the men they had married.

Sara held her phone to her chest, staring at the shadows stretching across the ceiling as she thought about making love with Greg. God, how she had loved that man. They had been sweethearts all through high school, and they had married soon after graduation. Greg had made her feel safe and secure. He'd made her feel cherished.

Now Landon, on the other hand, had brought out in her a pure, unadulterated horniness the likes of which she hadn't experienced in... *ever*.

Sara's phone trilled.

Heather: ?????

Almost simultaneously, Sara and Cathy answered.

Sara: Not the same.
Cathy: No. Not the same.
Cathy: As much as I hate to admit it.
Heather: ?????

Cathy: Sex is what Brad and I have on a pretty regular basis.

Sara: Cathy, I wouldn't call once every three months pretty regular.

Cathy: Shut up.

Bradley Henderson was a lifeguard during the summer season and he worked on the OC Emergency Medical Team the rest of the year. Cathy and Brad had dated, off and on through their teens. But then Cathy practically ran off with and married a man who had slowly but surely destroyed every bit of Cathy's trust in the opposite sex.

Cathy: Sex is what Sara is having with our handy plumber.

Sara: He's not a plumber.

Cathy: Farmer then. Sweet farmer fornication.

Heather: Cropman coitus?

Cathy: Exactly

Sara: :-/

Cathy: Sexual seeding

Heather: Tasteless Tillage

Sara: Stop!

Cathy: I'm sure it's both tasty AND tasteless.

Heather: Greedy gleaning.

Cathy: Steamy, hot harvesting.

Heather: Meadow mowing.

Cathy: Mucking the stall.

Sara: Okay, we're done. I mean it.

Cathy: Passionate plowing.

Cathy: Sorry. That one was too good to waste.

Heather: Sex with Steve was good.

Heather: But it was so long ago.

Heather: Was I having sex? Or making love?

Sara's heart pinched with pain for Heather. Six years ago, Heather had been wearing an engagement ring on her finger, and she had been right in the middle of planning her dream wedding, when tragedy struck and she'd lost everything.

Cathy: Don't be silly, hon. You were making love.

Sara: Yes. Not your fault Steve turned out to be an a$$hole of extraordinary measure.

Cathy: Spelled out clearly: he was a huge asshole.

Sara: Making love involves emotions.

Cathy: Emotions. *shiver* Dangerous territory.

Heather: It's been so long since I've felt...

Heather: anything.

Cathy: Liar. You feel emotions every day.

Cathy: Case in point – that kid who peed

the bed at the Lonely Loon this week.

Sara: Heather's head nearly exploded.

Heather: Don't you think the parents should have told me?

Heather: Had to have the mattress professionally cleaned.

Heather: Cost me a bundle.

Heather: Yes, I was angry. But I wasn't talking about that kind of emotion.

Sara: We know. {{{hugs}}}

Heather's self-esteem had taken such a hit when Steve dumped her, she'd built a wall of steel around her heart. She hadn't allowed another man to come anywhere near her for fear that she might be rejected again. Sara had hoped that time would heal her body *and* her heart. Her body had healed—even though Heather wouldn't agree—but her heart remained shattered.

Cathy: You need to follow my lead. Get yourself a bed buddy.

Sara started a text about Landon, but then deleted the few words she'd spelled out. Something felt wrong about making light of her... friendship with him.

Friendship? Was that the best adjective to describe what was going on between them?

He made her laugh. And when they engaged in serious conversation, he shared intelligent opinions and his attentiveness let her know he was honestly interested in what she had to say. She enjoyed being with him. In fact, he made her happy. He made her smile so often that, by the end of the day, her cheek muscles were often sore. Like a delirious monkey. She snickered.

Instead of mentioning Landon and risking more farmer sex ribbing, though, she decided to keep the conversation fun. Heather needed to be diverted from her dark thoughts.

Sara: We need to hook Heather up. Does Brad have a brother?
Cathy: Yes. Married with kids.
Sara: Bummer.
Heather: No hooking up. Seriously.

Sara knew Heather really was dead set against that idea. Her issues had roots that were deep and strong.

Sara: Heather, not every man is as shallow as Steve.
Cathy: R u sure, Sara?
Sara: You're not helping.
Heather: I'm going to sleep. 5 AM comes early.

Cathy: You got that right. Good night, my
    sistas!
Heather: See you in the morning.
Sara: Night.

On a sigh, Sara set her phone on the nightstand and studied the ceiling. Maybe Heather's heart *was* healing. The fact that she was wondering about the differences between making love and having sex with a man was evidence of a healthy interest. Maybe her curiosity would grow strong enough that she'd start dating again. Sara hoped so.

Like a slow, relentless rising of the tide, Landon seeped into her thoughts once again. The hug he'd given her out under the gazebo had taken her by surprise. A little burst of joy had exploded like a mini firework in her heart.

Cathy and Heather's teasing just now hadn't really bothered her. What did niggle at her was the strong compulsion she'd felt to shut it down. Her time with Landon was finite; she knew that. But for some odd reason, she couldn't bring herself to treat him like a passing thing or a seasonal fling. Their friendship — *their relationship* — wouldn't develop into anything serious. It couldn't. Not when he would be packing up and driving back to Kansas with little notice.

Still, her heart kept whispering that it

wanted him to mean something.

Sara turned onto her side, tugged the sheet up around her body, and did her best to ignore it..

CHAPTER NINE

HE HAD TO tell her. It was time. Actually, he should have been completely upfront with her days ago. However, his story was a strange one, and contemplating her reaction to hearing it had caused him to toss and turn every night since they'd nearly devoured each other at her shop. The explosively passionate encounter had been like nothing he'd ever experienced before. Episodes like that didn't happen to regular guys like him.

Landon absently stirred the spaghetti sauce that simmered on the stove, realizing that, when Sara turned her green gaze on him, he felt anything but regular. He tapped the large spoon against the rim of the pot.

How could seven short days alter his life so drastically? He drove into this town unsure of exactly why he had traveled out to the east coast, but each day that had passed since meeting this extraordinary woman gave him a peace like he'd never known. The calm seemed to have settled down deep inside him. Being with her felt... right.

Sara wasn't like any other woman he'd ever met. He hadn't laughed with anyone as much as he had with her. Her kindness and concern toward others had been proven in the great care and worry she showered on her mother, not to mention the time and attention she focused on her friends. Cathy and Heather were important to Sara. The three women enjoyed a deep friendship—a solid bond—that he truly envied.

He could hear Sara rummaging around in her bedroom down the hall. She was gathering more of her things to take downstairs to her mother's.

Landon had asked her if he could cook dinner for her, and he now opened a bottle of red wine. The cork made a small pop, and he set the bottle on the table so he could remove the cork from the spiral bottle opener. Today had been the first day they hadn't spent together; she'd been busy baking in her shop, and he'd made a trip to the hardware store, and then spent hours installing a shut-off valve under the industrial sized sink in Cathy's restaurant.

Sara was smart. A real entrepreneur. A person had to have a keen intelligence to run a successful business, and the mail order cookie venture she'd recently started showed her to be both ambitious and enterprising.

She had a brain in her head, that was certain, and she knew how to use it.

He'd learned real quick just how attracted he was to smart women.

Who was he kidding? It wasn't just her intellect he found appealing. The woman was gorgeous. Her green eyes were quick to sparkle with humor, and when she teased him, as she often did, he wanted to wrap his arms around her and kiss her senseless. Her golden blond hair framed her face in short, loose curls that invited a man to run his fingers through it. Dressed up in those short pants she wore, capris, he thought they were called, a t-shirt, and a baseball cap for a Saturday at the park, she was the epitome of cute. Decked out in a figure-hugging cocktail dress for an evening out on the town, she was an absolute stunner. She had curves in all the right places and they stirred some purely sexual images in his head that were, well, less than polite, to say the least. Yet, he refused to feel guilty about it. Hell, he was a man, wasn't he?

Brilliant. Beautiful. Sexy as hell. Sara was all these things and more.

Landon pulled two wine glasses down from the cabinet just as she entered the kitchen, carrying a small suitcase.

"It seemed easier just to pack a few outfits in this." She lifted the case a few inches, and then crossed the room and set it next to the back door.

He gave a doleful shake of his head. "I really should find my own space—"

"No more of that," she cut him off. "I mean it. You have no idea how much you're helping us."

His fingers curled around the bottle of wine and he arched his brows in question. She nodded, and he poured.

"I'm glad I worked on the plumbing today," he told her. "I've suffered through a few snippy remarks about my work ethic."

"You'll have to forgive Cathy." Sara accepted the glass. "She just can't help herself."

Landon chuckled. "How did you know it was Cathy and not Heather?"

"Because Heather has manners."

Sara grinned at him over the rim of her glass, her eyes glistening with delight, and Landon's heart *ka-chunked*.

"How was your day?" she asked.

"I finished up the install at Cathy's sink. I figured that would be the best way to get myself back into her good graces."

Sara's nod told him she agreed.

"She'll be ecstatic. In fact, tomorrow morning I expect her to serve you a double order of bacon with your breakfast."

The wine swirled into his glass when he tipped the bottle. "A man can never have too much bacon, and I don't know where Cathy gets hers, but it's extra delicious."

"She makes it herself every morning. The secret is brown sugar and fresh cracked pepper sprinkled on thick-sliced bacon, and then it's baked in a hot oven."

"I dream about those crispy little strips."

They both fell silent as they sipped their wine.

He glanced up at Sara just as she let out a deep sigh, her shoulders relaxing.

"I was so busy today," she said, "it was nearly quitting time before I had a chance to check the clock." She leaned her hip against the edge of the countertop. "I was surprised that you didn't stop in for a visit."

Landon lifted one shoulder. "Well, I knew you were baking. I wanted to... give you some space."

In reality, she'd been on his mind nearly every minute today.

She met his gaze squarely and said, "I missed you."

Those three little words sent joy zinging through him to the point that he couldn't contain his smile. "I missed you too."

Sara turned her head toward the stove. "That sauce smells wonderful."

"It's my mom's recipe." He hooked his thumb on his pocket. "She didn't teach me to cook, per se, but our kitchen was the gathering spot for the family. It's where we did our homework as kids. It's where my dad listened to crop prices on the radio, and where the family got together to talk about who would do which chores. I watched her cook this sauce so often, I guess I just learned how to do it through osmosis or something."

"Well, it has my mouth watering."

He watched as she swiveled around just enough to set her wine glass on the counter and then she approached him. Her chin dipped slightly and her green eyes turned darker with each step she took. She didn't stop until she was mere inches from him. He could smell the warm, flowery scent of her hair, and the muscles in his belly contracted.

"Then again," she whispered, "could be that it's not the sauce at all."

Landon offered her a languid smile.

They hadn't made love since the wild ride they'd both thoroughly enjoyed, but each time they were together, there was an acute underlying tension that tugged and toyed with them both. They liked it. Relished it. Savored it. He knew *he* did, anyway. Oh, hell, he knew she did too. Sara was attracted to him, and she let him know it with each enticing smile she offered him when she knew no one else was looking. The way she would gaze at him through her thick, lowered lashes completely bewitched him. But he hadn't acted on the attraction beyond hand-holding and a bit of kissing. He hadn't felt he could until he'd been completely honest with her.

She splayed both palms at the base of his ribs and slowly slid them up his chest. Something purely animalistic stirred to life inside him.

"Could be—"

Her wine-sweet breath brushed his jaw as she leaned even closer.

"—what's making me salivate has nothing at all to do with food."

Landon refused to look away from her beautiful face, blindly reaching out to set his glass on the table behind him and hoping it didn't crash to the floor.

"Let's say we turn off the sauce and have dessert first."

The sensuous drawl in her tone when she uttered the word *dessert* made his breath hitch in his throat. She slid her tongue across her luscious lips, and Landon's gaze became transfixed on her mouth. He wanted to taste her. Touch her.

She was so close, all it would take was for him to lower his head and he'd become consumed. But, no. They had to talk first.

His fingers slid over the backs of her hands and he forced himself to look into her eyes.

"Sara." His voice sounded ragged.

Her mouth curled at the corners, and she told him, "I'm not normally this shameless. But there's something about you, Landon, that puts me at ease. Something about the way you say my name that makes me want to..."

She leaned in to kiss him, but he quickly brought his hand up between them and gently touched her lips with his index finger.

"I know what you mean. I really do." He took her hands in his and roved over the hills and valleys of her knuckles with his thumbs.

"And there's nothing I'd like more than getting completely lost in some long, slow—" his lips quirked "—dessert."

"Good. I'm glad you like my idea." She kissed his thumb, then took it into her mouth, laved it with her tongue, gave it a gentle suck.

Landon grew rock hard, and for one, short moment, he considered putting off what he wanted to say; the thought of making hot, sweet love to Sara nearly overwhelmed his need to tell her what she so needed to know.

A soft groan erupted from his throat, a mixture of deep desire and even deeper regret.

"Wait, Sara," he said. She smelled like warm sunshine. Passion shadowed her eyes to a rich, mossy green. Her skin felt like hot silk, and all he wanted to do was strip her naked and smooth his hands over her body. But he couldn't. He just couldn't allow himself to surrender to his wants.

She began unbuttoning his shirt and kissed the vee of exposed skin on his chest.

He drew in a sharp breath; she'd drive him crazy before she was through.

Before he realized it, all the buttons were unfastened and her hands were on him, sliding on his waist and up his chest and... over his scar.

Sara jerked her hands away as if she'd

touched a live wire.

"I'm sorry," she murmured. "Did I hurt you?"

He dragged his eyes open and saw that she had backed up several inches, and although he'd lived with the remnants of his surgery for two years now, he felt his face grow hot as he straightened.

"No. Oh, God, no. I'm fine," he assured her, but even as he said the words, his gaze slid from hers.

What the hell? He'd never been self-conscious of his body before. In fact, he'd thought of his scar as a badge of honor. The operation hadn't just changed his life, it had *given* him a life.

However, no one other than his doctors had seen it over all these months. Sara was a woman he cared about. And the welted skin that ran nearly the length of his torso wasn't pretty. Her reaction mattered.

He forced himself to meet her gaze. "I'm all healed up. It just looks bad." Tension knotted in his gut tight as a boxer's fist.

Her shoulders rounded. "Oh, Landon. I've embarrassed you. I'm sorry. It doesn't look bad. Honestly. I was just... startled."

Her green eyes expressed her contrition; he wanted to let her know he was okay, but until he was certain she wasn't repulsed by the sight of him, all he could muster was a half-hearted smile.

"It's okay. Really." He began to button his shirt. "In fact, this is probably good. I've been wanting to talk to you about... some things. I want to tell you about... well... everything I've been through and..."

He let the rest of his disjointed, hacked up thoughts trail away. He felt suddenly enveloped in thick, dark clouds, like something bad was about to happen.

Even if she ended up thinking he was a lunatic, he had to tell her what was on his mind.

He heaved a sigh. "Can we go into the living room and relax? I really need to talk."

"Sure," she told him. "I'll turn down the sauce. Grab your glass and let's go sit on the couch."

"Just turn it off." Picking up both his glass and the bottle of wine. "It'll stay hot until we're ready to eat."

She turned toward the stove, but not before he caught a quick glimpse of her expression. Something bit into her brow and he couldn't say if it was mere curiosity or concern.

Once they were settled on the sofa, Sara shifted, bringing her bent knee up onto the cushion so she was facing him.

"So," he began, then he paused as he leaned forward and set his glass on the coffee table. He didn't need time to collect his thoughts. He'd lived with this story his whole life. Well, he'd lived with most of the story all his life.

He'd explained his health situation to every teacher, every youth fellowship leader, every friend he'd ever had. The newer parts, his most recent experiences since the operation—the oddest bits—he was not so used to verbalizing.

"What is it, Landon?" she finally asked. "Have you decided to go home? Are you leaving Ocean City?"

Her questions took him completely off guard. "No. Absolutely not. I like it here. I'm enjoying myself. Very much."

Relief had the tension in her face relaxing. She exhaled a little sigh.

"Oh, thank heavens. I thought that you might be feeling a little taken advantage of. I know working on all those old pipes and plumbing fixtures can't be easy."

"I don't feel the least bit taken advantage of," he assured her.

She nodded, and then pressed her lips together for a second before adding, "Have I been too... forward? Are you uncomfortable with—"

The small squeeze he gave her knee sheared off her sentence as cleanly as tin snips. "God, no, Sara. That's not what I wanted to talk about at all." He straightened and looked her square in the eye. "But it is *why* I want to talk. I like Ocean City." He pursed his mouth, then stressed, "I like *you*. A lot. It seems that we..." He licked his lips. "My feelings for you..."

Again, he stopped. Damn. He hated this uncertainty, this awkward hesitancy, but he was determined to get this out. If he had it wrong, she would straighten out his understanding quickly, he was sure.

"I meant what I said," he told her. "I like you, Sara. I like how you're always smiling. I like how you treat your friends, your mom, your customers. I like your ambition. I like who you are. I like that you enjoy everything you do, from baking all those delicious pies and cakes and cookies, to rolling up your pant legs on the spur of the moment and going crabbing in the bay."

She smiled at the reference. One day when they'd been out delivering desserts to a local restaurant, they'd made a quick stop at North Side Park so she could show him one of the town's many public docks. Somehow, conversation had turned to the bay's sea life, and when he'd teased her about her crab-catching abilities, she'd slipped off her shoes, rolled up the legs of her jeans, and waded in. When her hunt for a crab had ended unsuccessfully, she'd lured him closer to the shore with feigned, "ooh's and aah's" over something in the water he just had to see, only to splash him when he'd gotten into range. They'd both ended up laughing.

"I like that you're able to balance work and fun," he continued. "Not a lot of people know how to do that. Not where I come from, anyway." He inhaled fully; time for the honest confession. "I enjoy being with you. Very much. And I think you enjoy being with me."

Her smile widened, telling him unmistakably that what he said not only pleased her, but she also agreed with him. And it was as if the sun rose and warm, brilliant light chased away every nuance of darkness and doubt that had filled his chest.

"That's why I need to tell you," he said softly. "I need you to know a little more about me."

Her gaze gleamed and she leaned toward him just a bit closer.

"Okay," she told him, nodding her anticipation. "I'd like that."

Landon took a sip from his glass and then

set it back down. "I was born with several different congenital heart defects. The hole was easily repaired, I was told. But I had a valve that didn't work properly. My right ventricle was ill-formed, and my entire heart was weak... well, let's just say it was a mess."

As he listed off the anomalies, Sara's brows slowly drew together and she pressed the pads of her fingers to her lips.

"I grew up a skinny, runt of a kid," he told her. "I was allowed no heavy lifting, few outside activity, which is bad for a boy whose family operates a farm. Once I started school, there was no playground time for me, no sports. It was miserable."

"I'll bet." She actually looked pained at the thought.

"I did have a couple operations that I remember. The specialists were trying to make my heart work better." He chuckled. "Of course, I don't remember the operations, but I was old enough to remember the hospitalizations. And the pain. After I went into cardiac arrest on the table, though, my mother vowed there would be no more surgery. My symptoms were managed with pills after that, and I took a lot of them."

"How awful for you," Sara whispered. "So, no baseball? No football? No racing around the yard, playing tag."

He flattened his mouth and shook his head. "All of that was off limits. But my parents offered me as many non-physical activities as they could. We went to the library often, and there were always plenty of books around the house. I experienced a lot of fun and adventure right here—" he tapped his temple with his index finger "—in my imagination, thanks to some great authors. And there were video games to master and movies to watch."

"Still, though, it had to be hard."

He grinned, "I made out okay."

She lifted one shoulder in an if-you-say-so manner which made him laugh.

"Luckily, I enjoyed numbers," he told her. "Math was a favorite subject. My dad died before I graduated college, but before he passed away, he suggested that accounting might be a good way for me to help in the family business. By doing the books. So that's what I focused on during high school and that was my major in college. I was relieved to be able to finally earn my keep on the farm."

"I'm sorry about your dad."

Landon accepted her condolences with a slow nod. "He ran head-on into a cement abutment of a bridge near the farm. He was driving a new truck. Well, it was used, but it was new to him, so we don't know if he was fiddling with the radio or the heater controls or what, but something took his attention from the road."

Sara's head tilted to the side. "Oh, that's so horrible."

He took a moment to sip from his glass, but instead of setting it back down, he simply held onto it.

"My dad was a great man," he told her. "I looked up to him."

Sara lifted her glass and stared at the wine inside. "I wish I'd had a father I looked up to."

Landon questioned her with a silent gaze, but she shook her head.

She waved her free hand in the air. "That will wait for another time. You're the star of this story hour."

Her smile was excruciatingly sweet and her comment stirred his curiosity. He wouldn't forget to ask her to expound on it later.

"Right after my dad died," he continued, "my cardiologist suggested a heart transplant for the first time. He said I was a good candidate, and he reminded me that, being over eighteen, I could override my mother's refusal. But I just couldn't do it, Sara. My mom was still grieving for my dad, and I couldn't add to her stress. She'd have been riddled with worry and anxiety if I had pressed the issue at the time. And if something bad were to happen during the operation..." He just shrugged.

"So, life went on. I graduated college and took over the books and the ordering and finding local buyers. My life became busy and deeply satisfying, now that I was contributing to the family business. Mom hired Henry to do the physical labor, and he started dating my sister right off. Henry's a good man, and I always tried to respect him even if he didn't always return the favor."

His brother-in-law always saw Landon as weak, but he didn't have to get into those demeaning details. "My nephews arrived." He glossed over the intervening years; the story seemed to be taking forever. "Then Mom got sick. *Really* sick."

"Oh, Landon."

Sara's beautiful face pinched with sorrow.

"We knew she was hiding something from us," he said. "She began to look puffy and, well, just unhealthy. But we were shocked to learn that she'd gone into liver failure. From alcohol abuse." He looked out the window, but all he saw was darkness. "I knew Mom had a cocktail before dinner. Vodka tonic with lots of lemon was her drink of choice, but none of us knew how much she drank." He directed his gaze at

Sara. "I can honestly say I never saw my mom drunk. She didn't slur her words or stagger around the house. But she must have abused liquor for years." He lowered his tone. "Death didn't come easy for her."

"How sad," Sara said. "For her. For all of you."

"Almost immediately," Landon said, "my brother-in-law started talking about selling the farm. Needless to say, it churned up contention between us. My sister was on his side, of course. He made me feel... I don't know... lesser... weaker... because I wasn't able to help with the actual farm work. And I *was*, I guess. Lesser. And weaker."

He stared at the floor. Admitting that out loud had a rock-like knot forming in the pit of his stomach.

"Then Dr. Shultz brought up the transplant again, and I decided to go for it. I was told the wait could take years, but by that point I was just glad to be focused on something that would give me a little hope for the future."

"How long did you wait?" Sara asked.

"Only five months. Five months and five days to be exact. I couldn't believe it when the phone rang."

The memory had him smiling, and when he looked over at Sara, he saw that she was smiling too.

"That operation changed my life, Sara."

She smoothed her hand over his forearm, and up his biceps, the heat of her skin seeping through the cotton sleeve of his shirt.

"I can see that," she said. "A man doesn't develop muscles like these without some heavy duty workouts."

He grinned. "I spent months recuperating, and then more months in physical therapy. The stress between Henry and me worsened. But I was determined not to allow it to hinder my progress. I kept arguing with Cindy to give me time, that I'd be able to help out more, but she and Henry pushed and pushed. I fought them as long and as hard as I could." Quietly, he added, "We ended up selling, but you already knew that."

Deep commiseration softened her green eyes.

He shifted on the sofa. "I know I've taken way too long to tell you all of this and that you're probably starving but—"

"I'm fine," she told him.

"I'm just getting to the part I think you need to hear."

She set her glass on the end table and then directed every nuance of her attention on him.

"When I say the operation changed my

life," he said, "I mean that in so many ways. Physically, I felt so much better. I could lift bales of hay right just like every other laborer on the farm. Mentally and emotionally, I felt like a new person. It was as if I walked into that hospital one man and came out another. It wasn't over night, of course, but it was utterly amazing."

He rubbed his hand over his jaw before admitting, "There were other changes too."

Landon fell silent, and he feared that Sara would rush him.

She didn't.

"I started having these strange dreams," he told her. "I heard ocean waves and the call of seagulls. I felt the heat of the sun baking the top of my head. I would wake up in the morning and feel as if I'd spent all night walking in the sand."

He looked down and noticed that his fingers were curled tightly on the stem of the wine glass. He set it down, took a deep breath, and wiggled his fingers.

"I thought the angst dividing my family was causing it," he said. "Like, you know, maybe my mind was looking for some sort of refuge at night. Some sort of release. An escape. But... well... then it started happening during the day. I was wide awake, involved in tallying a long list of numbers and I'd hear this faint sound. And I'd realize it was the surf. A steady, rhythmic sound of waves. I thought I was going crazy."

"It doesn't sound all that crazy to me," Sara said. "Stress can do strange things to people, Landon. And you were under a lot of it. I mean, your mother passed away, you had major surgery, and your sister was pushing you to sell the family business when you didn't want to. That's called major stress."

"Yeah." He nodded. "I guess you're right."

The magnitude of his relief made his response come a little too quickly. He couldn't believe how well she was reacting to his odd experiences. Nobody back in Kansas had wanted to listen, let alone try to help him understand it.

"In the end, I decided it might be my sub-conscious urging me to just get it over with. To sign the damn papers and head for the coast. I swear, I felt like a volcano ready to erupt." One corner of his mouth tilted in a wry twist. "So I released the pressure. I worried that I had surrendered to Cindy and Henry. I still worry about that. But the relief was—" He tipped up his chin and let his head roll back and forth. "It felt so damned good to let it all go."

Sara eased herself up from the couch and

slid over onto his lap.

"I'm sorry for all the bad stuff you've gone through, Landon."

She trailed her warm, silky fingertips up and down the back of his neck. Her touch dipped beneath his collar and he closed his eyes.

"But I am so glad you found your way to Ocean City."

The scent of her was enough to drive him mad. "So you don't think hearing birds and the sound of waves is weird?"

Her lips slid into an erotic smile. "Maybe a little, but then I think everyone ought to dream about the ocean. The rhythm of it puts you in a deep, restful sleep."

She kissed him lightly on the mouth, and Landon wanted more.

"And you don't think," he whispered huskily, "my feeling so at home here is strange?"

"I think everyone would feel at home here. This is the best place in the world to live." Then she chuckled. "But I'm a little relieved that not everyone dreams about the beach. Because then we'd be overrun with masses of people all year long."

She kissed him again, this time longer, and deeper. Pleasure surged through him, thickening his blood.

She kneaded his shoulders and then delved her fingers into his hair, massaging his scalp with tiny circles.

He inhaled the scent of her, an arousing mixture of flowers and musk. He rested one hand on her waist, the other on her thigh, barely resisting the powerful urge to glide his fingers over the curve of her bottom.

Her wine-sweet breath brushed his temple as she trailed tiny kisses along his cheekbone, then ran her tongue along the outer curve of his ear. He hugged her tightly, sliding his splayed palms up the length of her back. God, she felt so good in his arms, all warm and soft. She looked so damned sexy. Her kiss tasted delicious. She smelled like heaven. Every sense was completely enveloped by her.

She arched her spine and sighed, her breasts pressing firmly against his chest; he could feel the hardened buds of her nipples through the fabric of their clothes. The sensation ratcheted the feverish need pulsing inside him.

Landon wanted to feel her bare skin, wanted to see her naked body, wanted to explore every silken curve, every secret furrow. He wanted her beneath him, wanted to slide into her, deep and slow.

The base of her ribcage was firm under his fingertips, but oh-so different from the firm fullness of her breast beneath the pad of his thumb. He salivated as he contemplated suckling the hard, honeyed nub. He inched a little higher and dragged his palm across her pebbled nipple. Sara shifted her hips, grinding herself against his lap as she softly moaned his name.

No one had ever spoken to him like that. Not a single woman had ever made his name sound so damned erotic.

"Now—" she was a hair's breath away, her moist lips brushing against his as she spoke "—*please*? I need that dessert."

He didn't have to be asked twice. He slid her toward his knees, then nudged himself forward and stood, lifting her in his arms. Her delighted squeal of surprise had him grinning.

"Your room or mine?" he said.

"Yours." Then she leaned in and began nuzzling his neck with kisses.

All his fears and doubts about his peculiar experiences melted away into oblivion, and all he could think about was making sweet love to Sara.

CHAPTER TEN

A PINKISH GOLDEN glow had just begun to light the horizon of the pre-dawn sky as Sara turned the key of her mom's front door and slipped into the house. She was a full grown woman who had been on her own for years, so she had no idea why she felt like a teen who had stayed out past curfew. Her mother wasn't the judgmental type. Still, she found herself turning the knob when she closed the door behind her to keep her entry as silent as possible.

Spending the night with Landon hadn't been her intent. But after *dessert*—that single word would forever hold a very different connotation—she and Landon had eaten dinner together. The sauce he'd made for the spaghetti had been delicious, but not half as luscious as their second round of dessert.

As she had lain in the warm cocoon of his arms, their legs entangled, the full length of their naked bodies touching, she hadn't felt so content, so safe, so satiated in... a very long time. She couldn't even remember if she'd fought off being lulled to sleep by the soft and steady rhythm of his beating heart.

Sara still had her back against the front door, lazily dreaming about how Landon made her body come alive, when she heard the distinct triple-meter beat of her mom slowly walking down the hallway with the support of her cane.

When Geneva entered the shadowy living room, Sara reached over and flipped on the light switch.

"Good morning," her mom said.

"I didn't startle you, did I?"

"No. I knew you'd be coming in. Heard you come down the steps outside."

Sara felt her face grow warm. "I'm sorry if I woke you."

"You didn't wake me, honey. I opened my eyes really early and realized I wasn't in pain." Geneva grinned as she made her way across the floor toward the kitchen. "I thought I'd better get up and enjoy every moment of this."

"I'm happy to see you're walking." Sara scooted around the coffee table. "Let me start some coffee. What would you like for breakfast?"

"Too early yet for me to eat," Geneva said. "But coffee sounds wonderful."

It wasn't long before the rich scent of Columbian dark roast wafted in the air and Sara and her mom were sitting at the table with their hands cupped around mugs of coffee laced with sweet French vanilla creamer, her mother's favorite.

"Did you have a good time last night?"

Sara simply could not contain the forceful grin her mom's question incited.

Geneva chuckled. "Please let me rephrase that. You said Landon was cooking. What did he make for dinner?"

"Spaghetti," Sara answered. "And it was delicious."

"I'm always impressed by a man who can cook." Her mom smoothed her hand across the glass table top. "Did you take something from the shop for dessert?"

Sara nearly spewed the coffee she'd just sipped. She swallowed quickly and reached for a napkin.

"No." Her lips quirked uncontrollably and she couldn't help adding, "He provided dessert too." She lifted the ceramic mug in an attempt to keep her mom from seeing the utter glee that seemed to explode inside her chest and on her face at the same time. But her smile continued to stretch until her lips were forced apart. Pure unadulterated happiness had her shoulders shaking with laughter she couldn't suppress. Her hands quaked and she feared she was going to slosh coffee onto the table. Sara set her mug down, pleased that she was able to do it before she'd made a mess.

Geneva lifted her hand, palm facing outward. "I'm not going to ask. And I don't want to know." But she chuckled right along with Sara.

After a few moments of silence, her mom said, "I love seeing you so happy."

"I am pretty happy." She placed the paper napkin she'd been holding onto her thigh and absently smoothed her palm over her, ironing out the wrinkles. "I'm a little scared too."

Her mom had always been a great sounding board; she'd always shown a great deal of patience when Sara needed to talk something through, and that was the case now.

"I mean," Sara continued, "I like Landon. And...well..."

She thought about his confession last night. He'd said those very words.

I like you, Sara. A lot.

"We enjoy being together. But…" She heaved a sigh. Sudden frustration had her snatching up the napkin and tossing it onto the table. "I feel this need to keep reminding myself to just enjoy today. Just like you always say. I want to take things one day at a time."

"You're saying you think there's no future for you and Landon?" Geneva asked.

For the span of several seconds, Sara didn't answer. Then she said, "First of all, I haven't known Landon long enough to even be thinking about this. I realize that. I really do. But for some reason…" The rest of the thought hung heavy in the air.

"Mom, when I married Greg, I thought that was it. I was sure we'd be together forever. And then—" She cut off her sentence with a quick swipe of her hand through the air. She didn't want to visit those dark memories today. "And then there's you."

Geneva started. "What about me?"

"Your love life, I mean. You and Dad were doing just fine. Then you get hurt and, *bam*, Dad's gone. Just like that."

The look on her mom's face had Sara reaching out and taking her hand. "I'm sorry," she rushed to say. "I didn't mean to bring that up. It's just that it seems relevant to what I'm going through here."

"I'm okay. It's okay. Really." She traced the outline of the mug handle. "You're only speaking the truth."

"The point is..." But Sara stopped and chewed her lip for a moment, trying to assemble her thoughts. "It's just that we don't know what the future will bring. Joy. Tragedy. And anything in between. Hell, *everything* in between."

"I can't dispute that," her mom agreed.

"Landon's home is half-way across the country. He did say he wasn't getting along with his family right now, but siblings squabble all the time, right? And they make up again. Sooner or later, he's going to want to go home." She looked into her mother's eyes. "And that makes me very afraid. I can't get too close to him. I don't want to get too... involved. I'm not up for a long distance relationship. And I'm certainly not moving to the mid-west and leaving you. I can't... I don't want to..." Fear made her throat go dry.

"Fall in love?" Geneva softly finished her sentence, and then she smiled. "Aren't you jumping the gun a bit?"

Sara pressed her palm to her chest and

shook her head. "I know. I know! It's *way* too early to talk about this. I mean, I've barely known the man for a week."

But even as she said the words, she wondered if that was really true.

"We would need a whole lot more time together before we talked about that." Who was she trying to convince? Her mom? Or herself?

Then her tone went all light and wispy. "Still, we really enjoy each other's company. We have so much fun together. He compliments me. Often. And that makes me feel so darn good. I think about him when we're apart." She whispered, "I like him, Mom." She clamped her lips closed, refusing to commit to anything more than that.

She tilted her head and sighed, her forehead bunching. "It's awful to be afraid of hope. This makes me happy. *He* makes me happy. But... what if something bad happens?"

Geneva touched her lightly on the wrist. "What if something good happens?"

Sara couldn't help but think about how badly she'd missed her father when he'd walked out on them, and about the bottomless well of grief she suffered when Greg died. There were times when she still ached from both losses.

"But, Mom," Sara said, "is the good worth

the bad?"

"Oh, honey, you know it is."

"Would you have married dad," she challenged, "if you knew he was going to walk out on you after you fell?"

"Absolutely," Geneva answered without hesitation. "We had a lot of good years together, Sara. I know you have good memories about your dad from when you were a little girl. So do I. He might have left me, but he gave me you. So stop talking like this."

Sara huffed out a sigh and shook her head. "I just don't want to... I don't think it's wise to..."

No matter how hard she tried, she couldn't finish the thought.

"I just want to enjoy the here and now." Then she tipped up her chin with determination. "I can't let things get too complicated. I don't want to hurt any more. I just want to have a good time while the good time lasts. That's not a bad thing to want, right?"

She knew full well what she was doing. All of this decisive thinking and planning was purely in the name of protecting herself. From heartache. From anguish. There had been enough of that in her past to last her a lifetime.

But even as she made the bold statement, a

tiny voice in her head told her it just might be too late.

"Honey," her mother's gentle voice drew her attention, "I know I go around telling everyone to enjoy all the good moments. And you should. But what you're talking about is something a little bit different. You're trying to rule your heart. And that can't always be done."

Sara reached for her mug, but when her fingers curled around the ceramic, she didn't take a drink.

"Oh, you can do all manner of preaching to yourself," Geneva said. "You can make all sorts of promises. But your heart isn't like a puppy. It can't be trained. You can't teach it to sit, roll over, stay. If your heart wants to wee on the carpet, honey, that's just what it's going to do."

She knew her mom's metaphor was meant to entice a smile, and it did.

"You're attracted to Landon, Sara. That's a fact. He makes you happy. Another fact." Her mother smiled. "All I'm saying is, you shouldn't try to wall up your heart. In the end, that's just going to cause you more harm than good."

Although Sara matched her mother's smile with one of her own, she crossed her arms under her breasts and remained silent.

"I just think it would be better if you didn't fight so hard." Geneva picked up her coffee mug. "Enjoy every good moment, yes. Grab hold of them and shake every ounce of good out of them that you can. By all means. God knows that's the only way I've survived. But don't shut yourself off from hope. And keep your heart open to every possibility."

CHAPTER ELEVEN

THE END OF October brought chilly temperatures with it that really settled in. Sara's clients had begun ordering more autumnal-style desserts—deep-dish apple and pumpkin pies flavored with cinnamon and nutmeg, her special pound cake laced with cardamom, hummingbird cake spotted with raisins and blanketed in a thick layer of cream cheese frosting, molasses cookies, dense, moist nut breads made with toasted almonds, pecans, or walnuts, and specialty cheesecakes.

"Mmmmm." Landon smiled as he swallowed the bite of cheesecake she'd asked him to sample. "Wow, Sara. This is delicious. I really like how you've sandwiched the pumpkin between the two vanilla layers. It looks as good as it tastes. And what's this crust made of? Graham crackers?"

"Ginger snap cookies. I crushed them into crumbs in the food processor. Add some ground walnuts, a tiny bit of brown sugar, some butter, and voilà, you have a great crust." She beamed at his compliment. He always made her feel so good about her cooking talents.

"You can say that again." He took another bite.

Watching him savor the cheesecake, Sara smiled. They'd had such fun together this month, searched out a different adventure each day. Yesterday was a prime example. He'd called her and asked her to meet him on the beach, and when she arrived, he was assembling a fancy kite he'd purchased at The Kite Loft. The blustery breeze made for perfect kite-flying conditions. After some trial and error, they both learned how to make the kite dip and sway, dive and soar. It had been such a simple activity, but she'd laughed so much her cheek muscles had become fatigued.

Landon blinked his long-lashed eyes open and leaned toward her. "Hey, I've got an idea," he told her. "Let's experiment."

Mischief danced in his chocolate brown eyes. She recognized that look, and a now-familiar heat curled through her like spiraling smoke as she anticipated what might happen next.

"I have a hypothesis," he said, his tone low and sexy. "I think the best way to mingle the flavors is to have a tasting buddy."

He swiped his finger through the bottom vanilla layer, capturing some of the sweet goodness, and then he slowly smeared it across her bottom lip. Then he did the same to the pumpkin layer, smoothing the dark orange filling across his lips. "Now," he murmured, waggling his eyebrows, "we taste."

She didn't know if she should laugh or lick the cheesecake from his mouth.

When they first made contact, his lips slid off hers, and she could feel the sweet goodness smear onto her cheek. But then he tried again, and his kiss was warm, and creamy, and spicy. Sara moved closer, sliding her arms around his neck. He tasted of pumpkin with a hint of cinnamon, nutmeg, and cloves, but she could also recognize the creaminess of the cheese, and the sweet vanilla too. Oh, and the ginger from the cookie crumb crust.

"Mmmmm." The sound vibrated from her throat.

When he broke off the kiss, she said, "Gosh, that is *so* good."

One of his brows arched. "The kiss? Or the cheesecake?"

She twisted around and took the fork from his hand. She raked the tines through the cake on his plate and cleaned them off against his closed mouth.

"The kiss, silly."

The fork clattered against the stainless steel countertop when she dropped it. Sara was certain she'd never tasted anything as sweet or as delicious as Landon's kiss.

She felt both his hands slide up her back so she figured he must have set down the plate. There was probably cheesecake and crust crumbs all over the counter, but she didn't care. The thought had her chuckling. This man had a way of making her care about one thing only—*him!*

He pulled back far enough so he could look into her eyes. "What are you laughing at?"

His chin sported a smudge of creamy filling, and she laughed as she reached up to clean it off with the pad of her thumb. "Nothing," she told him, licking the cheesecake from the pad of her thumb. "Nothing at all."

He held her in his arms and gazed into her face, his expression growing serious. "Listen,

I'd like for you to help me find an apartment."

She tilted her head. "Something wrong with our arrangement?"

God, how she loved having him upstairs. She hadn't realized how much she'd missed sex until he'd moved into her house.

"I need my own space," he said. "I have one more shut off valve to install in one of the bathrooms upstairs at the B&B, and then my job will be done. I'd like to stay in town a bit longer."

That news made Sara smile.

"And I've imposed on you long enough." He gazed down into her face, his tone suddenly saturated with a sensuous quality. "Unless you'd move upstairs with me."

It was a short sentence. Just half a dozen words strung together. But they caused a hard lump of something dark and scary to solidify in his chest, and before she knew what was happening, it was crawling all over her like a horde of scaly beetles, relentless and terrifying. She stepped out of his arms, backing up an inch or two, the edge of the counter hitting her at the small of her back.

"Oh, I... I don't think so, Landon." She tried not to frown, but she felt the muscles in her forehead tighten. "We, um... I, ah... I need to be careful about the choices I make. We need to take things slow. I need to make sure I'm doing the right thing."

Suddenly chilled to the marrow, Sara hugged herself, rubbed her hands up and down her upper arms.

"The choices we make are so damned important, don't you think?" She swallowed and moistened her still-sticky lips, the taste of nutmeg and vanilla distinct and pleasing and in sharp discord with the unexpected chaos that threatened to overtake her. "You really have to be cautious, you know?" Where had that pleading tone come from? "And then there are those choices life makes for you. Those can be utterly devastating. You're just going along, enjoying all the things you thought were safe and solid and permanent, and life just punches you right in the face, knocks you off your feet. Nothing is the same. Ever again."

Sara knew she was rambling, but she could no sooner stop herself than she could have stopped time or tide. "Life did that to me, Landon." She pressed her hand to the base of her throat. "You know I was married. Greg. My husband." Of course, he did. But the words kept toppling off her tongue. "Life just jerked him away from me. He was here one morning, and that same afternoon he was in a coma. Unable to speak. Unable to breathe on his own.

Just lying there. Unresponsive. And then he... He just... I was... I was..." She shook her head. "It was awful, Landon. I felt as if I were living in a pitch-black cave. Somewhere where the sun never shined. For months. I was desolate."

Her vision splintered as hot tears welled in her eyes. She thought she was over this, thought she'd put it behind her, moved past it, but the fear and the grief rolled through her just as fresh and horrific as the day she'd received the call from the nurse at the hospital about Greg's accident.

Suddenly, she was enveloped in Landon's arms. He gently guided her head onto his shoulder and kissed her temple.

"Sweet, sweet Sara," he whispered. "What is this about? I didn't mean to upset you, sweetheart. I was just teasing you. About moving in with me. You know... the mood felt right for lighthearted—" He flattened his mouth and shook his head. "I'm sorry, Sara. It was a stupid joke."

She blinked, and overwhelming emotion had her eyes welling with tears all over again. "It's just... just that... I..."

"It's okay. It's *really* okay." He slid his arms around her. "We don't have to talk about it anymore. Breathe and relax and smile. Everything's going to be all right."

Taking a deep, slow inhalation, Sara rested her head against Landon's shoulder and consciously let go of all the pent up stress in her neck, shoulders, arms, and face. Even her scalp felt tense. Another deep breath and she felt a little calmer.

"Forget about what I said, okay?" he told her. "It was a dumb thing for me to joke about."

Sara wanted to disagree. She wanted him to understand what she was feeling, wanted him to know that her anxiety was due more to her own insecurities than him. But her friendship with Landon—her *relationship* with him—was so mired in her dark, plaguing fear of loss and her need to avoid heartache; it was like a big ball of entwined rubber bands that couldn't be untangled without one or two snapping. How could she get involved with him with the risk of disaster striking at any time, bringing with it paralyzing grief?

Who was she kidding? She already was involved with Landon. Just because she didn't want to put a name to what was between them couldn't change that fact.

Shut up! she silently shouted down the annoying voice in the back of her head.

"How about this?" he said, his voice still a mere whisper as he slid a comforting hand up and down her back. "Let's just forget all about it, and you can help me find an apartment. Okay?"

Sara nodded, and then she tipped up her chin and gave him a light kiss on his jaw, hoping he would understand her silent gratitude.

CHAPTER TWELVE

LANDON SQUATTED NEXT to the pedestal sink and checked to see if he needed a right-angle stop valve or a straight one. He heard someone behind him and hoped it wasn't a guest staying at the B&B. They tended not to react too well when he told them they couldn't use the restroom facilities because the water to the building had been shut off.

He turned his head and swiveled on the balls of his feet.

"Hey, Heather," he greeted. "How's it going?"

"Good," she said. "I just folded these towels and need to put them away. It'll just take me a second and I'll be out of your way."

Between Sara's two best friends, Heather was the one he knew least. He spent most mornings in The Sunshine Grill, having coffee and chatting with Cathy and the locals. The time he'd spent with Cathy had helped him to recognize that there was anger beneath her brash tone. It was as if she were always on her guard, expecting to be hurt and lashing out with bold words so she could get her blows in first. He wasn't sure what had honed her edge of bitterness, but understanding her behavior had helped him not take offense at her impetuous, often flip, opinions.

Now Heather was an enigma, a mystery he couldn't quite figure out. Although she was always gracious, always polite, he got the distinct impression that she was uncomfortable around him, more so whenever they were alone. He couldn't tell if it was him, or just men in general. However, since he'd been working on the plumbing in the inn, they often found themselves forced into a bit of small talk. Heather was always friendly enough, but she could never quite look him in the eye.

She was a beautiful woman; her long brown hair was shiny and framed a creamy complexion and intelligent blue eyes. She always dressed nicely but conservatively.

Today, her pretty dress covered her from neck to ankles. It was clear to Landon that she tried to hide her voluptuous curves and wondered if she struggled with body image issues. No, Heather wasn't cover-model thin, but she was nowhere near obese, either. Self-consciousness about her weight could explain why she seemed nervous whenever they were alone. Then again, his conjecture could be completely off base.

He grabbed the pliers that were setting on the old, ragged towel he'd draped across the toilet seat. "Well, this is it. The last valve."

"Oh, Landon, that's great news." She set the towels on the small antique dresser. "I won't miss having to explain why the water's been turned off most afternoons. People on vacation don't like to be inconvenienced. Sometimes they can get a little snippy."

"I've run into a few of those myself." He grinned. Talking to her while squatting was causing him to crane his neck, so he stood up.

"I'm sorry if anyone was rude to you," she said. "I sure do appreciate all you've done." She focused on arranging the rolled up towels in the big basket that sat atop the dresser. "Sara told me you'd found an apartment."

"Yeah, it's a nice little place. One bedroom. A little kitchenette. I don't need much." He tapped the pliers against his palm. "She's okay with it, I think. Sara, I mean. With me sticking around town."

Heather grinned and glanced at him, although she didn't hold his gaze for long. She nodded. "Yeah, I'd say she is."

"You really think so?"

She stopped fidgeting with the towels and looked at him. "You really have to ask me that? You're with her every day."

Landon tipped his head to the side and offered a half shrug. "If anything was bothering Sara, you'd know it, right? You and Cathy are her best friends. The three of you are closer than sisters."

Heather nodded. "We are. Closer than sisters. We watch out for each other, that's for sure." She glanced down, shifted the basket full of towels a fraction of an inch. "Don't you worry. If Sara was unhappy, we'd let you know about it." She pressed her full lips together for a moment, obviously suppressing a grin. "One time back in high school, Sara got her hair cut for prom. She was going to surprise Greg. Well, he didn't like it and he said something mean. I don't even remember now what he said, but her feelings were hurt. She almost decided not to go, but we talked her into it. Why should she miss prom, we told her, because Greg was being an ass? They got through the night, but

Sara was hurt for weeks afterward, and Cathy and I made Greg's life a living hell."

Her shoulders shook with humor at the memory. "That poor guy. We chewed a whole pack of gum, piece by piece, and shoved those sticky lumps into the air vent holes of his locker. We soaped every inch of his car. He was furious. Oh, how he loved that Barracuda." She laughed out right. "And when he drove it to school the next day, all sparkling clean, Cathy and I skipped last period and smeared a can of shaving cream all over it. He couldn't see out any of the windows."

She tucked her hair behind her ear and then slid her hand onto her hip. "Even after the two of them made up, we continued to hassle him. We irritated the devil out of that guy. Sara asked us to stop, and Cathy and I both reminded her of how he'd made her cry. Finally, Greg apologized to *us*. He swore he'd never hurt Sara again. It was so funny. He was desperate to get back into our good graces, that's for sure." Heather crossed her arms as she got her grin in check. "The point to that story, I guess, is that, if Sara was unhappy with you, Cath and I would let you know."

Landon smiled and nodded. The story he'd just heard didn't sit well with him.

"So," he quietly began, "was Sara's

marriage a happy one? I mean, was her husband good to her?"

"Oh, absolutely." She nodded her head emphatically. "They were kids when that silliness in school happened. We all were; you know how immature teens can be." Heather smirked. "Greg proved to be a fast learner, though. He loved Sara very much. And she felt the same. They were very happy together. When he died, Sara was—"

She smoothed her lips together and closed her eyes. When she spoke again, her tone was very soft. "It was bad, Landon. Very bad. She was pretty much crippled by the loss she felt. And Greg's parents didn't help matters. Not at all."

"What do you mean? They didn't rally around her? Give her some support? She was their daughter-in-law."

"Well, Sara was the one doing the rallying," Heather said. "Naturally, they were as devastated as she. Once Greg had been pronounced brain dead, it took several days before Sara and Mr. and Mrs. Carson came to terms with exactly what that meant. Sara sat by his bedside, day and night. Once she finally got to the place where she was able to let him go, the doctor asked Sara about donating Greg's organs. Sara and Greg had talked about it, and she knew Greg would have been all for it. But his parents were dead set against it. Everything turned ugly, and there was terrible fighting."

She took a long, soulful breath. "Losing Greg was bad. But having her in-laws all over her like that just compounded the tragedy of it. I don't think they've spoken since."

"Sara went against their wishes?" Landon asked.

Heather nodded. "Yes. Sara donated Greg's organs."

They both fell silent for a moment or two.

"How long has it been..." he hesitated, "...since all this happened?"

"Two years."

Landon stared at the pliers in his hands, remembering how Sara had cried when she'd talked about her deceased husband. He knew he shouldn't ask, but he simply had to know.

"Heather, do you think Sara is over it?"

She paused for a long moment, then reached up and combed her fingers through her hair. "I think people never really get over that kind of thing. Losing a spouse, or a parent, or a cherished friend. It's not something you get over, is it? It's more something you learn to live with. Sara lost Greg, and she lost his parents, all in one fell swoop." She searched his face, then her chin dipped and she looked at the floor. "But I do think, for the most part, that Sara has reached the point where she's living pretty well with her loss. And I think that has a lot to do with you, Landon. You've helped her heal. You really have."

Warmth permeated his chest, coursing through his arms and legs, rushing to his face. Those words were good to hear.

"I hope she's healing, Heather," he said. "I really do. Because I'm pretty sure I've fallen in love with her."

Heather's shoulders relaxed and her face beamed with a smile. "Isn't this something you should be telling Sara rather than me?"

He tried to smile. He truly did, but he knew the twist of his lips only looked pained as he admitted, "I don't think she wants me to."

CHAPTER THIRTEEN

"WELL, WOULD YOU look at that bundle of preciousness?" Sara smiled as she watched the little girl approach her.

The child looked to be about four years old and she was decked out in glittering tulle from top to bottom. A bejeweled crown was perched on her head and she sported a scepter in her fist.

"Twick or tweat!" she called when she finally reached them.

Sara placed her hands on her thighs and bent at the waist so she was nearly eye-to-eye with the little girl. "You look so pretty." Then Sara smiled and waved to the girl's parents who stood a short distance away.

The child beamed. "My mommy buyed me this dwess." She pirouetted for them. Then the girl focused her attention onto Landon. "I'm a pwincess," she told him, the utter sincerity on her face expressing that she was certain he needed the explanation.

Sara bit her lip to keep from laughing.

"I can see that," he said. "And you're a beautiful princess too."

The little girl smiled even bigger.

Landon held out the basket filled with cookie pops.

She gasped, her eyes and mouth rounding with delight. "They're gigantic!"

Sara had baked large, ghost-shaped sugar cookies, decorated them with white fondant icing and used chocolate chips for the eyes, and then she'd inserted one extra-long lollypop stick into the bottom of each before wrapping them up in cellophane and tying the packages closed with black ribbon. The children, so used to receiving candy on this spooky night, seemed to love the cookie pops.

The little girl looked at her left hand, clutching the scepter, and then her right, holding her bag of treats. "Hey, mister," she blurted, "can you help me? My hands is full."

"I'll be happy to help you."

Landon took a cookie pop from the basket and tucked it securely into her bag.

"Fank you," she said, and then she turned and scurried toward her parents.

"Have a good time," Landon called after her. She stopped long enough to wave at him.

"This is fun," he told Sara.

Since dusk, local children had raced along the boardwalk, trick or treating in all manner of costume. There had been bloody zombies and famous movie and cartoon characters, ghosts and pirates, cowboys, a cute ladybug with pipe cleaner antennas, superheroes, a fierce dragon slayer with a long, plastic sword, clowns both scary and funny, and a cackling witch or two.

"I knew you'd like it." She leaned toward him, hugging his upper arm. "Thanks for being here with me."

"Are you warm enough?" he asked.

She rubbed her gloved hands together and nodded. "I'm good. You?"

He smiled down into her face. "I'm good too."

They'd shared some awkward moments since Sara had lost control and cried in front of him. He seemed to take great care in what he said and how he acted, but tonight the air between them felt light and fun. The Halloween festivities had a lot to do with it.

"Seeing all these kids dressed up and running around," he said, "makes me feel like I should have a few of my own. I think children would really alter your view of the world, don't you think?"

Immediately, he seemed to realize how what he'd said might sound. "Wait now," he rushed to assure her, "I wasn't making any suggestions—"

Her snicker cut him off. "No assumptions made." For a silent moment, she gazed out toward the ocean. The ever-present sound of the waves seeped through the night.

"I don't mind admitting that I'd like to have a few kids some day," she said.

Quietly, he replied, "You'd make a great mom, Sara."

She glanced up at him and he added, "No innuendos intended."

Humor made her mouth spread wide and she gave him a playful punch. "Would you cut it out?"

He laughed with her, but then his expression sobered. "So... why didn't you? Have kids, I mean."

"Oh, I don't know." She watched the group of children further up the boardwalk stop off at a business to get treats. "The time was never right, I guess. Greg was busy working. I was busy building my business." Then she grimaced and her voice dropped to a whisper as she revealed the full truth. "We thought we had all the time in the world."

Landon slipped his arm around her shoulders and gave a gentle squeeze. The silent seconds ticked on. He kissed her temple, and more silence ensued. Just when she thought she couldn't bear it an instant longer, they were besieged by a band of rowdy adolescents looking for treats.

"Yo, dude," the tallest teen, dressed as a 60s throwback complete with greasy, slicked-back ducktail hair, shouted, "trick or freakin' treat."

Four of the other five teens laughed, but one girl elbowed Mr. 60s in the ribs. "Would you stop being obnoxious? Not every Baby Boomer was rude. And they didn't all talk like a Brooklyn mobster."

Landon pressed his lips together to keep from grinning at the young lady doing the chastising.

"Don't flip yer wig, Amy," Mr. 60s said. "I wasn't being rude. Just trying to have a good time."

Amy just rolled her eyes.

One of the other girls squealed when she

saw the basket of cookies. Landon held them out to her.

"These are great." Dressed in a dirty prom gown that had been strategically torn to expose plenty of leg and half of her ample breasts, she had painted her face and arms with stark white crackle paint. The wide ribbon sash cutting across her torso labeled her Queen of the Dead. "I'm so sick of candy bars, I think I'm going to gag. If I eat all that chocolate my face is gonna break out."

Mr. 60s sniggered. "Is it hurtin'? Yer face, I mean? 'Cause it's killin' me."

Amy glared. "Har. Har. You're such a twatwad, Andy. Don't listen to him, Zoë. You look perfect."

Queen of the Dead flipped her long hair over her shoulder. "Keep it up, Andy, and you're going to get smacked."

Just then a fourth teen shoved her way toward Sara and Landon.

"Hey, can you guess what I am? Huh? Can you?"

Sara's brow knitted as she looked over the girl's costume. She'd have loved to take a guess, but she had no clue what the girl's costume might be. The brown lump that shot off her back was furry all over and had two legs protruding from the bottom, so it was obviously some sort of animal. However, Sara couldn't say if it was a goat, or a dog, or a donkey. A Guernsey cow, maybe? Hmmm. She glanced underneath. No teats.

"A unicorn?" Landon blurted.

The girl's shoulders fell and she huffed. "Do I have a horn on my face?"

"Did your doctor tell you that was a nose?" Mr. 60s needled her. "You should sue his ass."

The boys guffawed.

"*Andy!*" the other two girls shouted.

Ms not-a-unicorn narrowed her eyes at Landon. "I'm My Little Pony. Jeez."

One of the boys in the back said, "Let's saddle her up."

My Little Pony turned around and said, "You're driving me nuts with that, Donny. Cut it out. I mean it." But when she faced Sara and Landon again, the slight grin on her lips said she didn't mean it at all.

Sara felt it was time to move this crew along. She reached into the basket and handed treats to those who hadn't received one. "Have a great night, kids."

A couple of them murmured their thanks as they ambled on down the boardwalk.

Once the group of teens was out of hearing distance, Landon whistled and shook his head.

"Holy hell," he murmured. "Makes you

glad you didn't have any curtain-climbers, doesn't it?"

Sara leaned her head back and laughed. "Teens. The bane of every parent's existence." She reached out and touched his forearm. "Teens are the reason the universe makes babies so cute and cuddly and loveable."

"But they grow into *that*. Halloween or not, those boys were damned annoying."

"Oh, come on." She leaned into him, pressing her shoulder against his. "Lighten up. Teenaged boys can't help it; they're just at such an awkward stage. You don't remember what it was like? How exciting it was? Dressing up on Halloween, going out with the gang, annoying the girl who, in you heart, you really liked?"

"Nope."

His too-quick answer sort of snuffed out her humor.

"What are you talking about?" she asked. "You didn't tease the girls you liked?"

"I didn't go trick or treating."

"You're kidding me."

"Nope." He lifted his shoulders a fraction and let them fall. "I was sickly remember. And I lived on a farm. No neighbor for miles around. I wasn't strong enough to—"

"That is horrible," she proclaimed. "Absolutely horrible. No trick or treating? It's just *wrong*. I mean it. Terribly wrong." She glanced at her shop behind them. "Wait right there."

"Where you going? Don't leave me out here all alone. I'll be eaten alive by all these zombies and vampires."

Sara rushed into the shop and gathered a few items from the kitchen. When she returned, she was grinning.

"I have the perfect costume for you."

Landon groaned. "This really isn't necessary."

"Of course it is. Everyone needs to dress up at least once for Halloween. Here, take this." She handed him a rolling pin. Then she took the basket of cookie pops from him and set it on the boards. "Here, lean down a little." She tossed the white bib apron over his head, then wrapped the strings around his waist and tied it into a bow.

"But it has your name on it," he complained.

"Yeah." She nodded, then explained, "You're dressing up as me." Then she took the chef's hat from where it had been tucked under her arm and perched it on top of his head, fluffing it a bit so it stood up tall. "There." She planted her hands on her hips and looked him up and down. Perfect."

He smiled at her. "There is such satisfaction glittering in your eyes. You are one in a million, Sara. I mean it." He switched the rolling pin from his left hand to his right, never taking his eyes off her face. "You go out of your way to make life as perfect as possible for everyone around you. Do you know how rare that is?"

The way he was looking at her, combined with the compliment he'd just given her, made Sara's heart pinch with warmth.

"Hey," he said quietly, "I know you probably don't want to hear this, but I just have to say it. I love you, Sara. Now don't get upset. We can take things as slow as you need. But... I just had to tell you how I feel."

She stood there, hands on hips, smiling at him, and she tilted her head just a fraction. "I know I've acted crazy. So crazy that I have you second-guessing yourself all the time. I'm trying hard to get over it, Landon. I want to. I really do." She moistened her lips and nodded slowly. "Because I'm pretty sure I feel the same way about you."

Just then a little boy dressed as Spiderman marched up to them. "Trick or treat!"

"Here you go." Sara picked up the basket and held it out to him. He took a cookie pop and shoved it into his plastic pumpkin that was burgeoning with treats.

"Thanks," he told her. Then the boy eyed Landon, the frown biting his forehead a clear sign he was trying to figure out the outfit.

"You're a cook?" he asked Landon.

"I'm a baker." Landon raised the rolling pin so the child could see it.

His frowned deepened. "A baker? Named Sara?"

Landon slowly nodded. "Uh-huh. Exactly right."

Mini Spiderman just stared. Finally, he said, "I don't get it."

Sara laughed.

Landon said, "Neither do I, kid. Neither do I."

CHAPTER FOURTEEN

THE SUN BLAZED in the cloudless, cerulean sky baking the sand until it was too hot to touch with bare feet. They raced toward the shoreline, water splashing as they hit the shallows, and then he dove into a wave. He knew she wouldn't dive in, she'd just spent money having her hair done and would be loath to get her head wet.

Warm seawater enveloped him and foamy bubbles rushed over his skin in their race toward the surface. Opening his eyes, a murky blue-green world was revealed to him. The waves above rolled in on themselves, the current ruffling and tossing his hair as if it were a Gorgonian. Rays of sunlight shot like arrows through the water, creating pools of soft light on the ocean floor.

Then he saw her. Not all of her, of course, but her feet and legs were clearly visible to him. One side of her bikini bottom rose up to expose a little of her cheek and she reached around to snag the fabric and give it a tug.

Kicking his feet and propelling himself with one powerful stroke, he dove deeper as he approached her. He reached out and lightly pinched the side of her ankle, and immediately he heard the sound of her scream, muffled by the ocean around him. She lifted both feet, treading water and frantically trying to shift her position away from whatever sea creature— or so she thought—was nibbling on her.

His laughter shot a mass of air bubbles from his mouth and nose, and as he watched them rise, he could taste the briny water.

He placed his feet on the sandy bottom, bent his knees, and pushed toward the surface. He broke it and automatically flung his head back, centrifugal force clearing his eyes and hair of water.

The sharp call of a gull overhead pierced the hot, summer air.

Landon gasped awake, opening his eyes wide. He remained still, flat on his back on the narrow twin bed, his breathing and heartbeat racing as if he'd really just been swimming and playing in the ocean rather than having dreamt the experience.

The images and sensations felt so real he expected a white gull to be perched on a piece of his bedroom furniture and the bedding to be drenched in warm seawater, but when he reached out and smoothed his hand over the spread, it was cool and dry beneath his palm. The absurdity of thinking his room might have been invaded by a seabird didn't stop him from glancing around the room.

He threw back the covers, swung his legs out, and sat on the edge of the mattress. His bent elbows rested on his knees and he cradled his head in his hands.

What the hell? He felt like he'd lived that dream. But he'd never been in the ocean with Sara.

That *had* been Sara, hadn't it?

Who the hell else could it have been?

He padded from the bedroom and down the hall, unable to shake the feeling that he'd just run from the hot sand into the waves and dived, head first, into the ocean. That he'd peered through the greenish water. That he'd seen circles of sunlight on the murky sea floor. Even now, he could almost taste the saltiness of the water, smell the tang in the air. And that gull. It seemed the bird had swooped within a few feet of his head when he'd surfaced. He was sure it had been that piercing call that had awakened him.

In the kitchen, he pulled a glass from the cabinet and turned on the spigot. He guzzled down the water as though he were dying of thirst. He set the glass down, the sharp tap of glass against tiled counter almost made him flinch.

Landon moved into the tiny living room, reached for the remote control to the gas fireplace. With the press of a button, flames shot from beneath the fake logs in the grate and a welcome heat began rolling from the hearth.

Mid-November brought a sharp chill to the air, and he was grateful for the warmth of the fire. Besides, the dancing flames usually calmed him. Usually.

He sat motionless, striving to throw off the disquiet he felt as his unseeing gaze roved the room. He was only vaguely aware of the wavering shadows thrown by the golden orange firelight.

It wasn't as if the dreams were plaguing. They weren't unpleasant. Not in the least. To the contrary, in fact, the images and experiences almost always brought him a feeling of buoyancy, happiness, euphoria, even.

Until he woke up.

Once he was fully conscious, he couldn't shake the feeling that he was living someone else's adventure. Like he was eavesdropping or spying.

Like he was living in someone else's skin.

Landon leaned forward and picked up his smart phone from the coffee table. He unlocked it and tapped the screen to open an internet browser, and then he slowly thumbed out the letters g-o-r-g-o-n-i-a-n before touching the search key. He hoped he has spelled the unfamiliar word correctly.

"Also called sea whips," he read, "or sea fans, and are similar to the sea pen, a soft coral."

Why would he dream a word he didn't even know? Why, in his dream, would he liken the water flowing through his hair to a sea fan? He was from the Midwest. He came from a family that worked in the dirt. He knew crops. Corn and barley and hay. Wouldn't he have likened the experience to wind blowing through corn silk or through a field of wheat? Even in a dream state, wouldn't it be more natural for his brain to use metaphors he was familiar with?

Maybe he was possessed.

But he dismissed the asinine thought almost before it had completely formed in his head.

Unwittingly, he reached up and smoothed the flat of his hand across his chest. The bump of his scar made him go very still.

Maybe...

Sweat broke out on his brow and upper lip, and he felt queasy.

"No way." He said the words right out loud. Because he needed to hear them.

Then he remembered something Heather said to him.

"Sara donated Greg's organs."

Why hadn't he paid any attention to that news? Someone who'd had a heart transplant would normally take note of that kind of information. But he'd been too focused on finding out if Heather felt Sara was ready to move on after the death of her husband. He'd wanted desperately to learn that Heather thought Sara was ready to hear how he felt about her. That's where his attention has been centered.

Then he remembered that Heather told him Greg had died two years ago.

Two years ago.

Landon scrubbed an agitated hand over his jaw, chewing over these disturbing thoughts and correlations as if they were tough gristle.

The idea was beyond ridiculous. It was ludicrous. Completely insane.

But the dreams. His overwhelming desire to see the ocean. His feeling of finding home when he'd driven into Ocean City. His sense of familiarity when he'd first met Sara. No, it hadn't been mere familiarity. He had to confess; it had been complete and total déjà vu.

He shook his head forcefully, shoving himself up from the chair and pacing into the kitchen, then turning and walking back to stand in front of the fireplace.

This was crazy. This was demented. This was...

"Impossible," he murmured. "Absolutely impossible.".

CHAPTER FIFTEEN

SARA BLEW ACROSS the slice of pizza before taking a bite. Delicious, gooey cheese remained attached as she drew the crust away from her mouth. She chuckled and reached up to pinch off the string. Landon sat across the small table, lifting his bottle of beer to his lips. He gazed across the restaurant, looking to be a thousand miles away.

Ever since Halloween when they had both confessed their feelings for one another, Sara felt their relationship had blossomed. They'd already been spending a great deal of time together, but since that night they'd been nearly inseparable.

Heather and Cath had razzed her something terrible when she had forgotten about their November girls' night out. Landon had asked her to go to the movies and she'd accepted before remembering she had agreed to go out with them.

"You're choosing him over us," Heather had complained.

"It's not him, is it, Sara?" Cathy had jeered lightly. She wiggled her eyebrows up and down. "It's a part of his anatomy she's choosing over us."

Then they had laughed. The fact that Sara had assured them she intended to see the film with *all* of him only made them laugh even harder.

She and Landon had enjoyed the movie, and much later that same night, she had enjoyed *several* parts of his anatomy. Sara grinned even now at the memory.

Tonight, though, he'd seemed distant from the moment he'd picked her up at her place.

Finally, she reached out and touched his hand. "Hey, are you okay?"

He nodded, but it was an automatic reaction. Clearly, he wasn't okay.

"What's on your mind?" she asked. "Did something happen today?"

"Actually, it was something that happened

last night."

Landon tipped up his beer and finished it off.

"Where's our server?" he murmured. When he caught the young woman's eye, he lifted the empty bottle for her to see and pointed to it. She nodded and headed toward the bar. He slid the empty bottle next to the other one sitting by the salt and pepper shakers at the far side of the table.

"Eat some of your pasta," Sara urged. "It looks delicious."

"Not really hungry."

Sara frowned. "You had another dream last night?"

"Yeah." He ignored the plate of pasta primavera he'd nudged aside a few minutes earlier and laced his fingers tightly, resting his hands on the table. "Yeah, I did. And it was a doozy."

Her pizza forgotten, she asked, "It was a nightmare this time?"

"No." He shook his head. "It wasn't a bad dream. It was—" He shrugged. "It was quite pleasant."

She didn't know how to respond because she wasn't sure what the problem was. The dreams unsettled him, she understood that much. But if the dreams weren't frightening or threatening...

"In fact," he continued, "I woke up feeling happy."

The paper napkin felt especially dry when she rubbed it between her fingers. "Okay." She drew out the word a little. "So what's the problem?"

He seemed to study the cuffs of his sleeves, and rather than answer her question, he said, "I was swimming in the ocean. With you. I was under the water, and I could clearly see your legs, your ankles, your feet." His voice faded as he added, "Your toenails were painted bright red."

Then he lifted his gaze to hers. "I pinched you. Like a crab might. I made you jump and scream. I enjoyed myself immensely."

She rested her elbow on the table. "Sounds like fun."

"It was. The sun was hot and water was refreshing. I felt the air bubbles rushing across my skin when I dove into the wave. The fine-grained sand on the sea bottom was soft and cool against the bottoms of my feet."

The waitress brought his beer, and after thanking her, he took a long swig.

The thought entered Sara's head to warn him to slow down. Three beers on an empty stomach would impair his ability to drive. But in the end, she decided to keep mum. She would take his keys, drive him home.

Landon set the bottle down onto the table with a thump. "I don't have to tell you that you and I have never been swimming in the ocean together."

She smiled and tilted her head, her shoulders rounding. "We'll remedy that this summer."

Suddenly, she stopped and straightened her spine. The fact that she was willing to think in future terms where they were concerned said a lot. And the way the words had come out so freely, so easily. She hadn't given the idea a thought; she'd only voiced it as it had come to her. She'd have liked to explore this change in her thinking, but right now she felt the need to focus on Landon.

"Dreams come from your imagination, Landon. Just because you haven't done a thing doesn't mean you can't dream about it."

"But I don't think this is my imagination."

"What? Not your imagination? I don't understand."

Again, he stared at his entwined fingers and she could see the muscles in his jaw tightening and relaxing and tightening again. Whatever was on his mind disturbed him greatly.

"Not *my* imagination," he repeated.

His response only confused her further.

"I dreamed about coral. But not just any coral. Gorgonian."

"A sea fan."

He nodded. She almost teased him about the fact that everyone knew coral grew in the ocean, but his expression was so serious she feared he wouldn't appreciate it.

"I'd never heard of a Gorgonian in my life," he told her. "Why would I dream that word? And the coral wasn't even in the dream. I *thought* that word in my dream."

She reached out again, touched his forearm. "That does sound a little odd. But maybe you saw a National Geographic special or something?"

"Maybe," he muttered. Then he took another sip from his bottle. "I looked up some other stuff on the internet too. I went to Google, trying to find some information on organ transplant patients who have strange experiences."

The lemonade she sipped was sweet and delicious, but Sara barely noticed its taste when she swallowed a mouthful.

"One of the first terms I hit on," he told her, "was something called a chimera. That's a mythological creature that has the head of lion, the body of a goat, and the tail of a snake."

What did a mythological creature have to do with his strange dreams of the ocean?

"Chimerism is also a genetic term." Landon's fingers were still laced together, and now he pressed together the pads of his thumbs until his nails were bloodless. "Let me see if I can get this exactly right." He closed his eyes and slowly explained, "It's an organism that's composed of two or more genetically distinct tissues."

He went quiet, as if to give her time to absorb the information.

"Ah," she said, "so you being one, and the heart that was transplanted in you being another."

Landon's dark gaze met hers. "Exactly. Two genetically distinct tissues form something new. Something... different."

Sara squared her shoulders. "You think that chi-whatever-it-was has something to do with you?" She shook her head. "But you're not different. You're still you."

He didn't speak for several moments. She hoped like hell he intended to do more explaining.

"I found some other terms," he said. "Cellular memory and inherited recollection."

She frowned. "Cellular memory." She let

the two words roll off her tongue slowly, hoping like hell she could work out what he was getting at. "Inherited recollection." Finally she shook her head. "Inherited from whom?"

He didn't answer right away. Instead, he glanced across the room toward the front door, looking like he wanted to escape. Then he returned his gaze to hers.

"From the previous owner of my heart."

She studied his face. He was dead serious; she saw it in his eyes.

"Landon." Sara went silent. Then she couldn't stop herself from asking. "Do you know how crazy that sounds?"

His gaze never wavered from hers. "I do. Believe me. I know it sounds insane."

To keep from saying any more, Sara pressed the knuckle of her index finger against her lips and waited.

"I found all sorts of stories to confirm my beliefs," he told her. "There was a woman who had a kidney transplant who started craving Mexican food after her surgery. And not just any Mexican food. Enchiladas. She'd never eaten Mexican food in her life."

Sara gently raked her bottom teeth against her knuckle.

"The woman contacted the family of her donor," Landon said, "and learned that the young man whose kidney had been donated to her... well, he loved enchiladas. Ate them every chance he could get. Begged his mother to make them for him."

This sounded so outlandishly impossible. Sara wanted to laugh, but the fact that he was so resolute about what he was telling her made her feel jittery.

"There was another case I read about—"

"Okay, okay." She cut him off with a small swipe of her hand through the air. "I got it. I understand what you mean. But you want me to believe that the person who donated your heart lived near the seashore. Or loved the ocean. Or... or... was a fisherman." Her words came quicker and louder. "Or was a sailor in the Navy. Or an oceanographer."

Her skin felt flushed and her breath was coming in pants. She pressed her palm to the base of her throat. "Why am I so upset by this? I feel... angry. No," she quickly corrected, "not angry. Scared." She leaned toward Landon. "This sounds like it's straight out of science fiction and it's frightening."

She sat back, her chest heaving.

"There's scientific documentation," he told her quietly. "I can show it to you."

"No, thank you." With all this crazy talk, it was all she could do not to gather up her purse and jacket, scoot out of the booth, and head for home.

"Try to calm down, Sara," he said. "Because it's about to get worse."

The warning had her arching her brows.

Landon sighed and slowly rubbed his palms together. "You donated your husband's organs."

Sara was more than slightly taken aback. "How do you know that?"

"Please don't be angry with Heather for telling me," he said. "It's my fault. I was asking her some questions. About you. And it all just sort of came out. About the arguing. Between you and your in-laws."

Sara was back to feeling more than a little discombobulated. The mere mention of that awful time had black storm clouds stewing above her, threatening to drench her in dark memories. She shook her head in an effort to force the past from her mind.

"So how does Greg—" Finally, the picture came into sharp focus. "No." She said the tiny word emphatically. "What you're insinuating can't be. It's just not possible."

"I told you it wasn't just dreams," he reminded her. "I experienced this terrible longing to see the ocean." He reached up and raked his fingers through the hair on the back of his scalp, then scrubbed the same hand across the back of his neck. He took a deep breath before continuing.

"And I've had strong feelings of déjà vu." When he noticed how Sara was looking at him, he said, "I know this makes me sound like I've lost my mind. But I can't find an explanation that's more plausible. When I drove into this town, it felt like home. Really and truly." He swallowed and licked his lips nervously. "And that first day I met you, I felt it again."

His dark eyes narrowed slightly, and he looked like he had something else to say but seemed reluctant to say it.

"Then you fed me that cookie," he blurted. "And I knew that I knew you. That I had met you before. Somehow. Somewhere. That I had tasted something sweet—a cookie, a cupcake, something—from your fingers before."

He curled his fingers into fists and rested them on the table, his thumbs rubbing back and forth against the sides of his index fingers. "But I also know I hadn't. I hadn't met you before that day. I hadn't eaten anything with you either. I know I sound like a lunatic, Sara. But I also know how I felt at that moment. How sure I was that I knew you as I gazed up into your face and swallowed that cookie. And it scared the hell out of me, I don't mind saying.

So if I hadn't really met you before... then someone else had. And that someone led me here."

Landon just sat across from her, staring steadily.

The implications of what he was saying swirled around her and sent a creepy shiver coursing up her spine.

"But what you're expecting me to believe..." Her voice dropped to a whisper. "It's impossible. Absolutely impossible.".

CHAPTER SIXTEEN

"THAT SOUNDS SO—" Heather squinched her nose at the same time she reached for her second cupcake "—*strange.*"

Food was a comfort to Heather. Always had been. And this weird conversation was enough to upset anyone. So Sara slid the plate within easy reach.

"Yeah," Cathy agreed. "And it's not a good strange, either. This is something straight out of a Dr. Who episode."

Sara was still grappling with everything Landon had told her last night. As always in times of upheaval and turmoil, Sara had headed straight for the comfort and commiseration of her friends.

"I'd be more inclined to believe," Cathy said, "that Greg's spirit led Landon here."

Both Sara and Heather looked at her as if she'd suddenly sprouted a furry tail.

"Well, come on!" Cathy sat a little straighter in her chair, absently brushing crumbs from her fingertips. "Landon is trying to convince you that Greg's... what did you call it? Cellular thoughts."

"Memory. Cellular memory," Sara supplied.

"Landon is saying that Greg's heart tissue contains memories?" she asked. "And that those memories brought him here? All the way from Kansas?" She shook her head, her red curls bobbing. "That's just..."

Cathy searched for a word that fit and floundered.

"Ridiculous," Sara said quietly.

"Um-hm. That's exactly what it is." Cathy picked up her bottle of spring water, twisted off the top, and took a long swallow.

Sara swiped her finger through an errant dab of chocolate frosting on the plate and then licked her finger clean.

"I'll tell you what I think," Cathy proclaimed. "He knew. Somehow, he learned about Greg's accident. He found out about the organ donation."

"But that's impossible." Sara absently wiped her damp finger on the thigh of her jeans. "I asked that Greg's personal information remain sealed. You know I wasn't able to deal with that."

"Besides," Heather said, "Landon isn't that kind of guy."

"And, you, missy—" Cathy jabbed her finger toward Heather. "—are too gullible where men are concerned."

Heather actually laughed, but there was an edge to it. "Yeah, right, Cath. I'm gullible about *aaalllllll* the many men in my life."

"You know what I mean." Defensiveness laced Cathy's tone.

"No," Heather pressed, "I don't."

"Look," Sara said, wanting to avoid a quarrel between the two, "there is no way he could have known."

"Why?" Cathy asked. "Because you told the doctors to keep it secret? Too many people can't keep a secret, Sara. Not even to save their lives."

"But to what end? Why would Landon do something like that, Cath?" Heather lifted both hands, palms facing the ceiling. "It makes absolutely no sense."

"She has a point," Sara said.

Heather and Sara continued to look at Cathy. Finally, Cathy shrugged, "How am I supposed to know why? It's easier for me to believe he's up to no good than it is to swallow *his* explanation."

Picking up the knife, Heather cut one of the cupcakes in half. Smooth, creamy filling oozed out the side. "Landon wouldn't lie to you," she told Sara. "He loves you. He told me so."

"All the more reason for him to lie," Cathy muttered. "Don't get me wrong. I like Landon. He's a great guy. But he's either completely off his rocker, or he has one hell of an imagination."

Heather bit into the rich moist cake and chewed. "What you need to do, Sara, is request a list of Greg's organ recipients. That's the place to start."

Cathy nodded. "That's a great idea. Heather's right."

"Well, hot damn." Heather grinned. "Cath said I was right about something. I should get up and dance."

"But it's been two years," Sara said. "I wouldn't know where to start."

Heather swiped the corner of her mouth with a napkin. "Surely, the hospital gave you paperwork back then."

"Call the hospital administrator," Cathy

suggested.

"Or Dr. Ablang. Wasn't he Greg's PCP too?" Heather popped the last bit of cupcake into her mouth.

Sara nodded, her mind whirling. "I do remember that the organ donor program is run by a national network. Surely, it won't be too difficult for me to find it."

With a plan firmly in her grasp, Sara felt a little better. But it still didn't make Landon's story any easier for her to accept. Maybe, once she had proof that he wasn't on Greg's recipient list, she and Landon could begin to put this nonsense behind them.

But she had no idea what she would do if she learned that Greg's heart was beating in Landon's chest.

.

CHAPTER SEVENTEEN

SARA PARKED HER car at the curb and cut the engine, and although she pulled the key from the ignition, she didn't open her door. The peaceful scene beyond the windshield opposed the tension coiling inside her. It was that time of day when the sun had dipped below the horizon, yet the sky wasn't quite dark. The street looked deserted; the clouds to the west had turned a deep purple-gray. The phragmites growing at the end of the street swayed with the light bay breeze.

The sealed envelope sat on the dashboard. She still marveled that she'd had the willpower not to open it. The mail carrier delivered it earlier that afternoon, and she'd spent an hour or more vacillating between wanting to get the task over with and avoiding it altogether. But then her curiosity began to blaze like an oven set to broil and all she wanted to do was tear open the envelope and finally learn the truth.

But in the end, she decided it would be best if she opened it with Landon. He had just as much at stake in this as she. However, now that she'd arrived at his apartment, dread became as paralyzing as steel shackles.

She hadn't seen Landon for ten long days. She'd called to let him know she intended to request the names of the transplant recipients, a conversation that had been extremely short. After that, they hadn't talked on the phone. They hadn't exchanged texts. It was clear that both of them needed some space.

It had taken all this time for her to finally receive the information she was after. She'd started by searching the medical bills for the name of the doctor who had been in charge of Greg's care in the ICU. The physician had put her in touch with someone from the hospital administration office who had promised to contact the United Network of Organ Sharing on Sara's behalf. After forms had been signed and calls had been made, Sara had waited. And waited.

One thing she could say for certain... she had missed Landon. Fiercely. She couldn't even count the times she'd reached for her phone, a smile on her face and butterflies in her chest, intending to text him about something funny that had happened. At least twice, she'd had the entire message typed on the screen, her thumb hovering over the send button before she remembered the terrible mess they were in. And late at night. God, how she'd longed to call him to ask about his day and tell him about hers, or ask him some inane question just so she could hear the sound of his voice.

With her mom and Heather and Cathy around her, she could never really describe herself as being alone. But without Landon, these past ten days had seemed to drag by, minute by drawn out minute, and there had been times she'd ached with loneliness.

She hoped he wasn't on that list.

But what were they going to do if his name *was* there among the other recipients? Uneasiness crept over her skin.

Immediately, she told herself for what felt like the thousandth time how absurd this was. Of course, his name wouldn't be on that list.

Then she frowned. If she was so certain of the outcome, why had she stayed away from him? Her stomach went queasy.

Damn it! Just get it over with already!

She reached toward the envelope, but

before she touched it a gentle knock on her driver-side window gave her a start. She looked to her left and saw Landon standing by the car. The engine was off, so she fumbled with her key ring for several seconds before she was able to ram the key into the ignition and turn the power to auxiliary. The window slid down.

"Are you okay?" he asked.

Her expression must have been strained, because he said, "Did something happen to your mom? Are you all right?"

For just a fraction of time, Sara's stress was forgotten; his concern for her mother and for herself had her mouth curling into the tiniest of smiles.

"Mom's good," she assured him. Then tension came flooding back. "I have the list."

"Oh." He'd been bent over at the waist, but he straightened his spine and the reusable grocery sack he carried made a little whooshing sound when the fabric brushed against his trousers.

Sara could see the rectangular boxes of several frozen dinners and one end of a roll of aluminum foil. His other purchases were hidden by the bag. The thought of lecturing him about eating too many processed foods wafted through her mind, but she ignored it. Now wasn't the time.

"So what are you going to do?" he asked, deadpan.

She had to lean to the left to see his face. "Open it?"

"You haven't opened it?" His surprise was evident. "You want to come inside?"

Flattening her mouth, she shook her head. Quietly, she asked, "You want to come sit in here? I'll turn the heater on."

"I don't need to see." His tone was firm. "My gut is telling me my name is on that list. My gut, my dreams, my heart—"

"Landon, please. Just get in the car. It's too chilly to leave the window down." Then she murmured, "I could use the support."

He hesitated, and then he took two steps away from the car and set his bag down on the sidewalk that led to his apartment. Sara watched him round the nose of her car, open the passenger-side door, and get inside.

"How have you been?" she asked him.

Swiveling his head, he narrowed his eyes at her in the gloom. Her question sounded forced, almost fake, with that elephant of a white envelope taking up such a huge amount of the space between them. But the question had been all too real. She wanted to know, had been wondering about him since they last saw each other, and once they read that list, who knew if she'd have another chance to ask about him?

"I'm good."

He licked his lips, and she remembered the soft touch of his kiss on her mouth, her neck, her shoulders, and other, more secret places on her body. Her heart thudded against her ribs.

"I volunteered to deliver meals to shut-ins," he said. "This past Tuesday was my first day." He glanced out the windshield ahead. "I enjoyed myself. Made me feel like I did something good."

Sara nodded, but she couldn't have offered him a smile even if she'd wanted to. She was too busy trying to figure out why this information gave her such a sense of relief. And then realization struck; his volunteering efforts seemed more an act of someone setting down roots than they were of someone preparing to leave town.

Suddenly, she was acutely aware of the quiet that surrounded them in the interior of the car. Her fingers and toes were chilled, and she remembered that she'd promised to turn on the car's heater, but she hadn't. However, instead of reaching for the ignition to fire up the engine, she gave the overhead light a one-finger punch and plucked the envelope from the dashboard.

UNOS was printed clearly in the upper left

corner, her address typed out in the center. She stuck her finger beneath the glued flap and ripped, leaving behind ragged edges that mirrored her nerves.

The papers felt brittle between her cold fingers, the small bulb in the car's ceiling throwing a pale yellow light across the interior of the car. She scanned the cover page and quickly let it fall to her lap. Looking over at Landon, she saw that he was motionless, barely breathing as he stared straight forward, waiting.

The list was long, and Sara's lips parted in silent surprise as she read. Bones, marrow, blood and platelets, kidneys, liver, intestines, veins, tendons, inner ear tissue, corneas. Heart. There it was. Greg's heart...

...was flown by air transport to Kansas. Received by Landon Richards.

Emotions eddied inside Sara. First and foremost was fear. To think that Landon had somehow been altered by the operation, and that something had led him here. To her. It was just too freaky to be believed.

Tears welled, burning her eye sockets and blurring her vision.

"Oh, my God," she whispered. "It can't be. It just can't be."

A fist-sized lump swelled in her throat,

cutting off anything else she might have wanted to say.

Landon chose that moment to look at her, and Sara knew she hadn't yet gotten a handle on the terror that churned and rose and threatened to drown her.

"You knew, didn't you?" Her accusation was as sharp and rusty and dangerous as oxidized nails. "How did you know?"

He said nothing, his jaw muscles tensing to cords, and then he shoved his way out of the car. Landon didn't cross in front of the car to the sidewalk where his grocery bag sat. He walked down the center of the deserted, dead-end street toward the bay.

Glancing down, Sara saw that her hands were trembling so badly that the paper was steadily tap-tap-tapping against the steering wheel, and then she caught sight of herself in the rearview mirror. She saw a reflection of what Landon had just witnessed—her absolute horror. Naked and garish.

A fat tear seeped from one of her wide-open, red-rimmed eyes and ran the length of her face. All at once, she realized what she'd done.

"Oh, God," she groaned. She tossed the list onto the passenger seat and flew out of the car. "Landon, wait." But he didn't stop, he didn't even slow down, and she wondered if he'd heard her. She called his name again, hurrying to catch up with him.

By the time she was close enough to grasp his forearm and bring him to a halt, they'd nearly reached the end of the road, the wooden barrier meant to block cars from driving into the marshland barely visible through the thick, brittle overgrowth of reeds.

"I didn't mean that," she cried. "I wasn't calling you a liar."

"Sure sounded like that was exactly what you were saying."

He was right, and she couldn't refute it.

"I'm sorry. It was the shock, I guess. I didn't mean it. You know I didn't mean it. I thought I was ready. I guess I wasn't."

There was a sharp edge to the chill in the air that stung her eyes, making them water. The tangle of her emotions didn't help. She reached up and dashed the tears from her cheeks, the pads of her fingers as cold as tiny cubes of ice.

"Landon, I didn't mean it," she repeated for the third time.

He didn't look convinced in the least.

"How can you be so damned calm?" Her question gushed forth like carbonated bubbles rising toward the surface of a fountain drink, in a mad rush and completely unstoppable.

She watched both his shoulders lift in a small shrug.

"I've had more time to live with the idea."

Sara couldn't tell if his response was a question or a statement. Her brow furrowed. "But it's so unbelievable. How could this happen?"

He stuffed his fists into his trouser pockets. "You have to find a way to deal with this, Sara. It's like the weather. Back in Kansas, we had to learn to live with whatever the sky gave us. There were always surprises. Always too much of something and not enough of something else. Too many clouds, not enough sunshine. Or too much sun and not enough rain. Or, surprise! Here comes a tornado. You deal with it. Asking a bunch of unanswerable questions is a waste of everyone's time."

His little spiel rubbed her the wrong way. "That would be fine if we were talking about when to plow the back forty, or how best to rotate the crops—" she jutted her chin forward, her tone intensifying "—*or the price of corn*, Landon. But we're not, are we?"

It didn't take a fancy college degree to understand that her question was purely rhetorical, so she wasn't surprised when he just stood there, silent and as still as if he were made of stone.

"We're talking about... *Greg's heart*..." Speaking those last two words made her voice break. "Beating in *your chest*."

The small flame of anger that had flared inside her just a moment before fizzled, and disquiet seeped through her veins like icy winter seawater, causing her to shiver.

"It's... it's..." She shook her head, holding her hands out in front of her. "Bizarre doesn't even begin to describe this. It's scary. It's unnatural." She shoved her bangs off her forehead. "And it makes me want to run as fast and as far away as I can."

His dark eyes simmered as he narrowed his gaze. His jaw was clenched tight and his nostrils flared.

"Then run, Sara," he told her. "Run fast and run far. Get as much distance as you can from the *bizarreness* of it all. But me?" He poked his index finger to his chest, hard. "I don't have the luxury, now do I? I'm forced to deal with reality. I have to come to terms with what is. Strange or not, I don't have a choice. Because I can't live without the heart that's pumping blood through my body."

He turned away from her then, marched off along the street, stepped up onto the curb, and walked along the sidewalk. She stood in the street, watching him. He picked up his bag and disappeared behind a thatch of pale ornamental sea grass planted at the corner of the neighboring property.

The street looked as empty and as barren as she felt inside. Slowly, she became cognizant of the sound of the tiny waves lapping against the marshy shoreline and she turned to stare at the bay. But the wide expanse of cold, inky water offered no comfort..

CHAPTER EIGHTEEN

"Don't be surprised if she's pissed," Cathy told Heather. "That's all I'm saying."

Sara and her mother entered the bright and airy kitchen of the Lonely Loon, their hands filled with contributions to the gathering of family and friends for the annual pot-luck Thanksgiving dinner. Savory fragrances filled the air. Geneva hobbled into the room on her own, and a relieved Sara smiled but couldn't help herself from sticking close to her mom's side for support should she be needed. Thank goodness, her mom was having a good day.

"Who's going to be angry?" Sara asked. "And why? What hot gossip have we missed?"

Heather had whirled around to face them at the sound of Sara's voice, the soap bubbles clinging to her hands proof that she was in the middle of doing some washing up. She immediately reached for a tea towel and rushed at them, delight brightening her face.

Several moments were spent in greeting. Cathy and Heather both had hugs and cheek kisses for Geneva, and a glass of deep red merlot was thrust into Sara's hand once she was able to unload the yeast rolls and boxes of desserts she'd baked.

"This needs to go into the fridge." Geneva handed the bowl to Cathy.

Sara had been so self-focused for the past few days that the holiday had sneaked up on her. She wouldn't have given Thanksgiving a thought had her mom not asked earlier in the week if the pot-luck dinner was still on their calendar. Sara hadn't really felt in the party mood, and she'd considered staying home, but her mom had awakened feeling so upbeat and pain free this morning that she'd been able to shower and dress herself for the special occasion. She'd even put together a bowl of ambrosia to bring along.

Knowing how infrequently her mom felt this good, Sara just couldn't dash Geneva's happy anticipation by canceling out on the get-together. Besides that, she knew that being with Heather and Cath would lift her spirits and help her to forget her miseries, at least for a few hours.

She savored the wine's fruity richness and smiled at the smooth finish. "Wow, that's good."

"Could I have a little?" her mom asked Cathy.

"Of course." Cathy turned to pull a glass down from the cabinet.

Sara was surprised by the request. "Mom, are you sure?"

"I didn't need a pain pill today," Geneva told her as she settled onto one of the Windsor chairs. "So I'm sure I'll be just fine." Then she instructed Cathy, "I just want a little, hon. To celebrate."

Heather reached for her wine glass that was sitting on the rectangular table among the bowls, measuring cups, spoons, a couple of onions, nuts, spices, a bag of fresh cranberries, and other ingredients.

"To friends and family." Heather lifted the glass, and everyone followed suit.

After swallowing another sip of wine, Sara asked, "So who were you talking about when we came in?" She reached across the table and pulled a walnut half from the bag. "Sounds like we interrupted a juicy tale."

"Not as juicy as that ambrosia salad." Cathy bent at the waist and gave Sara's mom another hug. "Geneva, you *are* going to give me your recipe this year, right?"

"Oh, honey, it's nothing special." But the request had the older woman beaming.

"The turkey, stuffing, and sweet potato casserole are all in the oven on warm." Heather glanced around the kitchen as she focused on ticking off the dishes on her fingers. "Mashed potatoes and succotash are on the stove. The cranberry sauce is in the refrigerator."

Cathy caught Sara's eye and they shared a grin, proclaiming in unison, "We love your cranberry sauce."

And they did. Heather's recipe included mandarin orange slices and walnuts, and it was delicious.

"Sara, you brought the rolls?" Heather asked.

"Of course," she assured her, "and dessert. As requested. But what about the juicy gossip?"

"Cathy, if you'll get me a pen and paper," Geneva said, clearing a small space in front of her on the table, "I'll write down that recipe for you."

"Sure thing." Cathy spun toward the far corner of the kitchen where she knew Heather had a junk drawer loaded with Post-it notes, pens, pencils, paper clips, duct tape, a flashlight or two, and myriad other paraphernalia.

"Why do I get the feeling that no one's listening to me?" Sara's eyes narrowed. "Hey, were you talking about *me*?"

"Heather," Cathy said breezily as she plunked a stubby pencil and a piece of paper in front of Geneva, "it's okay if I put some music on, right? And the table still needs to be set."

The sound of the old brass knocker being tapped against the front door made all of them pause.

"I'll get that," Cathy rushed to offer.

"Wait." Sara snagged the sleeve of Cathy's sweater, bringing her friend to a halt. "How come you didn't tell me you invited your special friend?" Sara teased.

Cathy's spine seemed to arch in offense and she raised her brows. "That's because I don't have a *special friend*. And, besides, Brad is spending the holidays with his mom in Florida." She tugged her sleeve from between Sara's fingers. "I need to answer the door."

After she disappeared, Sara called after her, "If you don't have a special friend, then how'd you know who I was talking about?" She was still grinning when she swiveled her gaze to Heather. "So who's joining us?"

Heather had piled her long dark hair onto the top of her head in a loose bun. A few curling tendrils framed her face and she'd accentuated her brown eyes with a little mascara and liner. But no amount of makeup could disguise her expression; she looked like a kid who'd gotten caught swiping her finger through the cupcake icing.

"You *were* talking about me." Dread swirled in Sara's belly as she whispered the accusation. "Please don't tell me you invited Landon."

Heather swiped the back of her wrist across her damp forehead and slid into the chair, leaning forward in supplication. "It's one Thanksgiving dinner, Sara. He doesn't know anyone in town. He'd have spent the whole day all alone."

Sara just gave her a narrow-eyed stare.

"He helped us so much," Heather tried again. "I realize that you two—"

"How could you?" Her mouth had gone so dry, she had difficulty saying those three little words.

"She didn't," her mother said. "I did."

"What?"

"Sara, you're going to have to get over yourself sooner or later." Her mother met her gaze, head on and unflinching.

She couldn't have been more shocked had her mother smacked her cheek.

"Get over myself?" Sara said when she finally found her tongue. "How can you say that when you know what happened? We talked about it and talked about it."

"Ad nauseum."

The comment stung like a second slap and Sara actually gasped.

"I'm sorry, honey," her mom said. "I went too far there. I shouldn't have said that. I'm happy to listen whenever you need me to."

The apology didn't do much to heal her wounded feelings. "I told you how the whole situation creeps me out. It's scary."

"And I'll tell you what's truly scary." Geneva scooted her chair a little so she could look her daughter directly in the eye. "Facing an uncertain future of taking care of your physically disabled mother when your father has packed his clothes and walked out. Now, *that's* scary. And you, my strong and brave girl, never faltered. Not once."

The woman reached out and grasped Sara's hand in hers. "And I'll tell you what else is scary. Going head to head with two stubborn, selfish people who wanted to bury their son, whole and intact, when you knew in your heart that's not what your husband wanted. *That* is scary. You were fearless. You held your ground and you did what you knew was right."

The mention of Greg, and knowing Landon would be sitting at the dinner table, made Sara's stomach go queasy. She swallowed and murmured, "It's just not... natural. The way he was led halfway across the country."

"It's perfectly natural," her mother snapped. "You stick a white chrysanthemum into a vase of blue water, and what happens? The flower petals turn blue. It's an easy concept to grasp. Everything has its effects. Everything."

"But he dreams about the ocean." Sara had already explained all this to Heather and her mother and Cathy, *ad nauseum* as her mother has described. But she couldn't stop herself from repeating, yet again, "He admitted that, the day we first met, he'd known he'd already met me."

Calmly, her mother said, "A part of him had."

"And you don't find that strange?"

"Look, Sara, I'm not saying it's not peculiar. I'm just saying it's not as odd as you're making it out to be. For the love of sweet Jesus, you've got to suck it up already. Get over yourself. Show a little courage. Be nice to the man while he's here. That's all I'm requesting. Just for today, honey. Tomorrow will take care of itself."

Strains of Landon's deep voice carried to the kitchen from the foyer. Sara couldn't tell exactly what he was saying, but her heart rate accelerated and she felt as if someone had turned up the setting on the thermostat.

Geneva waggled her index finger in fine, listen-to-me-I'm-your-mother fashion and lowered her tone as she added, "Try to remember the good times the two of you had together. Think back. Before you discovered the odd bits, Landon made you smile. He had a good effect on you. You can't deny it."

That's when Cathy re-entered the kitchen with Landon close on her heels.

"Hey, everyone," Cathy called in a bright voice, "look who's here."

Even though there were only five adults gathered in the B&B's kitchen, the room felt crowded. Sara watched and listened as her friends and her mom did their utter best to create a celebratory atmosphere.

Landon caught her eye and offered her a single, silent nod. Relief flooded her when her smile didn't fail her. It might have been small, but it was a smile.

He looked at Heather, who had gotten up

from the table and now stood near the stove. "I brought wine." He held up two bottles. "I wasn't sure how many people you were expecting, or if you'd want white or red, so I brought a bottle of each. And if we run out, there are two more bottles in my truck."

Cathy raised both hands into the air and let out a cheer that had him laughing.

"You can set those on the buffet in the dining room, if you don't mind," Heather told him.

"I'm on it."

He'd no sooner left the room and Cathy turned her suddenly fretful gaze onto Sara. She whispered, "Don't be mad. Are you mad?"

Sara pushed her chair back and stood up. "What do you think?" She started for the door. "I'm going to get this over with."

"That's my girl." Pride brightened Geneva's tone.

"You could set the table," Heather suggested. "Plates and cutlery are already out there."

As Sara left the kitchen, she heard Cathy hiss, "I told you she'd be pissed. Holy hell, she'll make us pay for this through Christmas, I just know it."

The last comment nearly made Sara chuckle to herself. It wasn't so much that she was angry. She knew their intentions were good. But she did feel a little betrayed. Someone should have told her. However, even as the thought entered her head, she had to admit that, had she known Landon had been invited, she'd have stayed home. So it was for the best that the news had been kept from her.

To reach the Loon's formal dining room, Sara had to pass through the breakfast room where guests enjoyed morning coffee or hot tea and the light, continental fare Heather offered. If they wanted something more substantial, they went downstairs to The Sunshine Grill. The B&B was empty this week as most people preferred to spend the holidays with their families. But it wasn't unheard of to have guests staying at the Loon over Thanksgiving or Christmas. During the few holidays where that had happened over the years, Heather simply invited the guests for dinner, cooked a larger turkey, and added the table extension and extra chairs.

When she entered the dining room, she saw Landon standing at the far side of the room, his hands in his pockets as he gazed out the window. She cleared her throat softly to let him know he wasn't alone.

He turned, and he immediately smiled. "Hey."

The greeting was warm and relaxed, and it set Sara at ease.

Landon took a couple of steps toward her, stopped behind a tall-backed dining chair, and curled his fingers around the dark-stained wood. "Are you okay with this?" he asked. "My being here, I mean."

She nodded, uncertain if her silent response was the truth or a lie.

He looked so good, so damned handsome. His smile made her heart sing, but just as quickly, she remembered how he came to be here, in Ocean City, at her shop, in her home— *in her bed*—and awkwardness began to encroach on the moment.

Her lips were dry as beach sand and she moistened them with a quick glide of her tongue. "Help me set the table?"

"Sure." He reached for the stack of plates.

The silence between them quickly niggled at her as she rounded the table, setting a water glass at each place setting. Landon, too, ambled around the table, placing a plate in front of five of the chairs.

"I'm surprised that you're here," she said. "What I mean is, I'd have expected you to go home to Kansas. To be with your family."

He lifted one shoulder. "There's no home in Kansas anymore," he reminded her. "I did call my sister." He tilted his head and screwed up his mouth. "Things between us are better, but still strained. She still believes her husband did the right thing; I still feel annoyed." He smiled across the table at Sara. "I'm sure we'll be fine. We just need more time."

Sara wondered if that's all *she* needed. With enough time, could she learn to live with the strange events that brought Landon to town—*to her?* Maybe, but she seriously doubted it.

"Oh, I found a job."

"You did?" She didn't even try to hide her surprise. Employment in a tourist town during the off-season was hard to find.

"Yeah, I was talking to a guy in the hardware store just down the road," he said. "I guess I must have wowed him with my vast array of knowledge."

He chuckled at his boastfulness, and so did Sara.

"Come to find out, he's the manager, and he offered me a job right there on the spot."

In silent agreement, he took the job of placing the linen napkins beside each plate and she arranged the cutlery. They worked well together.

"It's just part time," he added, "But it gives me something to do four days a week. And I'm going to continue delivering meals to shut-ins."

"I'd have thought you'd get a job as a plumber's assistant."

They laughed, and then Landon grew serious. "I'm glad you're okay. I've been worried."

"I'm okay," she assured him, and this time she knew she was telling him the truth.

"Let's get this party started!" Cathy came into the dining room, her hands filled with bowls.

Heather was right behind her, carrying side dishes as well. "We have enough food to feed everyone on the block."

Sara grinned. "That's what I love about Thanksgiving."

Her friends looked relieved that she was smiling and she rolled her eyes at them.

Soon everyone was talking at once.

"Landon, open the wine."

"I'll put on some music."

"Someone pull Sara's rolls out of the oven!"

"Bring the salt and pepper shakers when you come back."

Geneva appeared in the doorway, clutching the jamb, and Sara rushed to offer her mom some help to the table. "Don't forget my ambrosia."

"No worries. I'll get it, Mom."

When the meal was finally on the table and they were taking their seats, a stranger stood in the doorway at the far end of the room, the entrance from the front foyer.

All of them were startled by his sudden appearance. Cathy actually let out a little squeal.

"I knocked," the man said, and then he added, "twice. The door was unlocked so I let myself in."

Sara saw that he carried a suitcase in one hand and had what looked like a messenger bag slung over his shoulder, something used to carry a laptop.

"I have a reservation."

As if in some sort of comic synchronism, all of them turned their heads at the same time to look at Heather.

The man looked at her too. "I assume you're in charge."

It was obvious she was flustered, that she wasn't expecting a guest to show up. Finally, she spoke. "You're Mr. Atwell?"

"Yes," he said. "Call me Daniel."

Heather rounded the table. "You're early. Four days early. Your reservation is for the first of December."

Sara glanced at Cathy to see if she knew this guy was coming; Cathy shrugged and gave the tiniest shake of her head.

"My agent made the reservation," Daniel told her. "He must have messed up the dates. Can you accommodate me?"

"Of course." Heather clasped her hands in front of her. "It's no problem. But there will be an extra charge for the extra days."

"No problem." Daniel Atwell peered around Heather, his gaze quickly touching everyone. "I was hoping for peace and quiet. I'll be working. I was told I'd be the only guest."

"And you are," Heather assured him. "We're celebrating Thanksgiving. Would you like to join us for dinner?"

"No." Then he asked, "Could I get a key? And I'll let you get back to your meal."

"Sure. Follow me." Heather quickly pivoted in a half circle. "Cathy, would you carve the bird? Everyone sit. Relax. I'll be right back in a few minutes."

And with that, the two of them disappeared.

"Did she say anything to you about a guest?" Sara whispered to Cathy.

"Not a word." Cathy picked up the knife and began slicing into the breast meat.

Geneva's eyes gleamed as she leaned in. "You know who that is, don't you? DB Atwell."

Landon said, "The author?"

The older woman nodded. "Doesn't he remind you of Heathcliff? Dark and brooding... and delicious?"

"Mother!"

Not thirty seconds after leaving the room, Heather returned, folding a check in half and tucking it under a candlestick on the side table on the way back to her chair. Atwell's footsteps could be heard as he made his way upstairs.

"I was so busy prepping for dinner," Heather said, a little breathless, "I didn't get a chance to tell you. I got the call last night. He's paid for two months. In advance. Not for just his room, but for *all of them*. I am sitting pretty for the entire winter."

Her excitement had everyone smiling.

"Okay, let's make a toast," she ordered. "We should eat before everything gets cold."

Landon lifted his hand, palm out. "Do you mind if I do the honors?"

Heather just smiled and nodded.

He picked up his wine glass and so did everyone else. He cleared his throat.

"First off, I'd like to thank Geneva for inviting me today, and Heather for opening her home to me, and Sara for being okay with my being here. It means a lot to me."

"Hey, pal," Cathy said, "what about me?"

"And to you, Cathy," he quickly amended

his toast. "For making the best bacon on the face of this earth."

Cathy wobbled her head back and forth, preening at the compliment. "You got that right."

They all chuckled.

Landon paused, sobering. "Now I don't mean to make anyone uncomfortable with what I'm about to say, but here goes." He raised his glass. "This is the first time that I've ever had a chance to say thank you and have it really mean something. I wish I could thank Greg for all that he's given me, but since that's impossible, I want to thank all of you. You knew him. And loved him. I'm sure it's no surprise that I want to thank him for changing my... for *giving* me a life."

Sara dipped her head and stared down at the napkin draped across her lap.

"Before my operation," Landon continued, "I merely existed. But now I'm strong and fit. I can hike and lift and dance the night away. I can enjoy living like never before. And for that, I'd like to make a toast to Greg."

Geneva responded with a soft, "Hear, hear."

"But there's another reason I need to thank Greg," he said. "For loving his wife."

Sara's mouth parted in silent surprise and

her gaze flew to Landon. His chocolate brown eyes bore into hers, holding her captive with breathtaking intensity.

"Greg loved you so deeply, so completely, that his feelings for you somehow permeated the very cells of his body. His loving memories continue, even though he can no longer be here with you, Sara. Through some miracle, I sense them, I *dream* them. And long story short... I'm here... in Ocean City because of him. And I am deeply grateful."

Landon's eyes glistened with emotion. "I can't explain it. No one can. But because of Greg, because of my transplant, I met you. And I found out first hand why he loved you so much. I'll be forever indebted to him for... more than I can possibly put into words. Even though things didn't work out for us, Sara, I hope that we can still be friends. I want you to know I wouldn't change a thing. Not a single thing."

After the toast, the bowls of food were passed around. Wine glasses were refilled. Silverware tapped against good china. Soft music played and conversation was made. The B&B's new guest was discussed, and Sara was vaguely aware of Cathy doing a bad imitation of the man by proclaiming, "I was hoping for some peace and quiet."

But Sara felt as if she floated through the entire meal in a fuzzy haze. All she could think about was Landon's toast. Oh, she had realized he was grateful to Greg for the organ donation. From the list she'd received, Greg had saved half a dozen lives and enhanced the lives of others.

Landon had been utterly precise when he'd talked about Greg's love for Sara. And she had loved her husband just as much. Deeply and completely. Greg might be gone, but Sara would never forget him or what they'd had together.

What her relationship with Landon had taught her, though, was that she still had room in her life for affection, for fun, for romance—*for love.*

With the voices of her family and friends buzzing around her, Sara was struck with a stark revelation: her heart cried out for Landon.

Cathy and her mother laughed loudly, snapping Sara to attention. She chuckled, not because she was enjoying whatever joke was being told—she hadn't a clue what they talked about. Her stupid grin was because she felt suddenly light as a seagull feather inside.

"Where did Landon go?" she asked.

Rather than answer her, Heather teased,

"What's got your head in the clouds?"

"Daydreaming about DB Atwell?" Cathy snickered.

"You, missy," Sara told Cath, "have had enough to drink."

"Landon's in the kitchen," her mother told her.

"He's clearing up the table," Heather said. "So we can have dessert."

"Yeah," Cathy quipped, "Sara won't give him any *sugar*, so he'll have to settle for Snickerdoodles and pumpkin pie."

The raunchy emphasis she put on the word 'sugar' had Heather howling. Even Geneva was grinning, and shaking her head.

"Keep it up," Sara warned, not quite able to rein in the humorous quirk of her lips, "and I'm going to let loose on you."

"Ooooo." Cathy's eyes went wide in mock horror.

Sara got up from the table. "I'm going to go make some coffee."

"To go with those *Snickerdoodles*?" Heather batted her eyelids.

"And *pumpkin pie*?" Cathy laughed so hard she snorted.

"Mom," Sara murmured as she was leaving the room, "guard that wine bottle, would you?"

Geneva *tisked*. "Oh, now. They're just

having a little fun."

"Yeah, at my expense."

In the kitchen, Sara stood in the doorway, watching Landon rinse the plates and stack them in the dishwasher.

Her mother had been right. He had changed her. He had given her a hand out of a deep hole she hadn't even known she'd been stuck in. He'd made her world better. Brighter.

And all those things he'd said about Greg... well, Landon had just about melted her heart.

In that moment, she knew. Without doubt. She loved this man. Loved him *hard*. And she would let neither fear nor crazy-ass circumstances keep her from letting him know that.

Doubt and anxiety and near-panic and every other manner of negativity had caused her to waste enough precious time. She couldn't say what the future would bring. No one could. But she wanted to grab onto every moment of happiness she could, and she intended to start right here, right now.

With sureness in her step, she started across the floor toward him.

Her movement caused him to look her way and he grinned. "Sounds like the party's gettin' a little rowdy in there." He bent to place a saucer in the stainless steel rack.

"Yeah," she murmured, stopping just a foot or so way from him, "and it's about to get rowdy in here too."

"Huh?" He straightened quickly, his elbow smacking into two pot lids, sending them skittering across the counter and crashing into the deep sink. "What'd you say?"

Sara ignored his question. "Landon, what you said in there—" she tilted her head toward the dining room "—during your toast, was beautiful."

...his feelings for you somehow permeated the very cells of his body.

Just remembering his praise of Greg made Sara's knees go weak all over again. And Landon's perspective changed her whole outlook on the transplant, the dreams, and his strong sense of déjà vu.

He just stood there, his sleeves rolled up to reveal his forearms. God, she just wanted to sink into him, feel his hands wrap around her, bury her face in the curve of his neck. But she had a few things to say first.

"The last time we were together," she began, "outside your apartment, you were calm and rational and logical. But I wasn't ready for any of those things."

Landon nodded. "I know you weren't. And it's okay."

She languidly wet her lips. "But I'm ready now."

"Really?"

"Uh-huh, really." She closed the gap between them, splayed her palms on his chest. His muscles felt warm and firm beneath her fingertips. "Is that okay?"

His mouth cocked in a sexy half-grin. "Oh, it's more than okay."

Sara leaned in and kissed him on the jaw. She slowly became aware of the thud of his heart beneath her palm, and she inched back far enough to gaze at the back of her hand. The rhythm beat strong and steady.

And she felt no fear. No disquiet.

She did, however, experience a poignant hitch of emotion that made the love she felt for this man deepen just a little more.

"I love you," she whispered.

His throat convulsed when he swallowed against the sudden emotion that softened his gaze. "I never thought I would hear you say that. I love you too, Sara." His voice grated roughly as he repeated, "I love you too."

He searched her face for only a moment, then bent his head to kiss her. He gathered her up in his arms and crushed her to him in a tight hug.

"Whoopsie!"

Landon broke off the kiss, but the two of them continued to hold one another as though they'd come to a silent agreement that they'd wasted enough time apart. They glanced across the room.

Heather and Cathy stood grinning in the kitchen doorway.

"Looks like Geneva isn't the only one wanting a *Snickerdoodle*." Heather sang the name of the cookie in off-key notes.

Cathy cracked up. "Sorry to interrupt you two, but we want dessert."

Obviously, she was anything but sorry.

"It's okay," Sara told them. Then her tone lowered to a hush as she warned Landon, "Never let them see you sweat. Or they'll become relentless."

"Gotcha," Landon said. "Let's show them just how okay it is."

He kissed her then, deeply, thoroughly, and Sara felt her pulse race even though they had a half-drunken audience looking on.

"Woo-hoo!" Cathy cheered. "Forget the cookies. They're going straight for the pumpkin pie!"

Sara and Landon laughed so hard they had to stop kissing. She hugged him to her. Holding him felt good. It felt right. And Sara knew they really would be okay.

A NOTE FROM THE AUTHOR

I hope you enjoyed Following His Heart. If you did, please consider leaving a review and telling a friend about my book. Good reviews and word-of-mouth recommendations are an author's best means of finding new readers. I thank you from the bottom of my heart.

I don't know anyone who has had an organ transplant, and I don't know exactly how the UNOS system works. I may have bent, mangled, and/or broken some of the rules of this wonderful system in order to make the situation between my characters work. I meant no harm.

I urge everyone to become an organ donor.

Those who do can save up to eight lives and enhance the lives of many others through tissue donation. In the USA, registering to be a donor is done on a state by state basis.

Click your state at OrganDonor.gov...

http://www.organdonor.gov/becomingdonor/sta teregistries.html

...to find out more!

RECIPES

Writing Sara's story was fun for me because I have such a love of cooking and baking. As soon as the weather turns chilly, I can be found in my kitchen, baking breads, cakes, cookies, and pies. I'm always on the lookout for a new recipe I haven't tried, and I often post my successes on my blog:

http://www.DonnaFasano.com.

The following are a few recipe favorites from the women featured in *Following His Heart*.

Sara's Yeast Rolls

Makes 24 rolls

1 (1/4 ounce) package active dry yeast
1 cup warm water (110º-115º F)
1 teaspoon sugar
1 egg
2 tablespoon extra virgin olive oil
1 teaspoon salt
3-4 cups all purpose flour

1. In a small bowl, dissolve the yeast and the sugar in the warm water. Let sit until frothy, about 10 minutes.
2. Add egg, oil, salt and 2 ½ cups of flour. Beat until smooth. Stir in enough of the remaining flour to form a stiff dough.
3. Turn out onto a floured surface and knead until smooth and elastic, about 8 minutes. Place dough into a greased bowl, turning once to coat. Cover with a kitchen towel and let

rise in a warm place until double in size, about 1 hour.

4. Punch dough down and turn out onto a floured surface. Divide dough into half. Divide each half into 12 equal-size pieces.

5. Roll each piece into an 8 inch long rope. Tie each rope into a loose knot, tucking under the ends. Place 2 inches apart on greased baking sheet. Cover the sheets with kitchen towels and let rise until double in size, about 30 minutes.

6. Pre-heat oven to 350° F. Bake rolls for 15-18 minutes or until golden brown. Remove from baking sheets to wire racks. Serve warm with butter.

Geneva's Ambrosia

Serves 8-10

1 (8 ounce) container whipped topping
2 cups shredded coconut
1/2 cup walnut pieces
1 (8 ounce) can fruit cocktail, drained
1 (8 ounce) can pineapple tidbits, drained
1 (11 ounce) can mandarin orange slices, drained
2 cups mini marshmallows
1 (10 ounce) jar maraschino cherries, drained and halved

1. In a large bowl, gently mix together all ingredients until well-combined. Stir gently; orange slices are delicate. Refrigerate for at least 1 hour before serving. Can be made a day ahead.

Sara's Snickerdoodles

Makes about 2 1/2 dozen cookies

2 1/2 cups all-purpose flour
2 teaspoons cream of tartar
1 teaspoon baking soda
3/4 teaspoon salt
1 cup butter, room temperature
1 1/2 cups sugar
1/2 teaspoon vanilla
2 large eggs

Coating -
1/4 cup sugar
1 1/2 tablespoons ground cinnamon

1. Whisk together the flour, cream of tartar, baking soda, and salt. Set aside.
2. Beat the butter, sugar, and vanilla until light and fluffy, about 4 minutes. Add eggs, one at a time, and beat until well incorporated.

Scrape down the sides and bottom of the bowl.

3. Add the flour mixture to the butter mixture in three batches, mixing each addition just until the flour is mixed in. Do not over mix or cookies will be heavy. Wrap the dough in plastic wrap and chill for 30 minutes.

4. Pre-heat oven to 400º F. In a small bowl, mix together the coating: 1/4 cup sugar and 1 1/2 tablespoons cinnamon.

5. Shape tablespoon-sized mounds of chilled cookie dough into balls (or use a medium size cookie scoop). Roll each ball in coating mixture and place 2 inches apart on baking sheets. Bake 8 – 10 minutes or until puffed and set. Cookies should be light golden. Cool on baking sheets for 10 minutes, and then remove to a cookie rack to cool completely. Cookies will keep in an airtight container for 4 – 5 days.

Heather's Fresh Cranberry Sauce

Makes 8 – 10 servings

2 12-ounce bags fresh cranberries
1/2 cup water
3/4 cup orange juice
1 1/2 cups sugar
1 teaspoon cinnamon
1/2 cup walnut pieces
1 15-ounce can Mandarin orange slices, drained

1. Place cranberries in a 2 quart pot. Add water, orange juice, sugar, and cinnamon. Simmer, stirring often, until all cranberries have popped, about 20 minutes. Remove from heat.
2. Gently stir in walnuts and orange slices. Pour into a serving bowl and chill thoroughly. Best made a day ahead.

Cathy's Brown Sugar &
Cracked Pepper Bacon

Makes 9-12 strips

1 pound thick-sliced bacon
4 tablespoons dark brown sugar
Fresh cracked black pepper to taste

1. Pre-heat oven to 350º F. Line a jelly roll pan or roasting pan with foil. Pan should be large enough to hold a cookie cooling rack. Place the cookie cooling rack on the foil-lined pan and brush the rack with a little oil to prevent sticking.
2. Lay bacon on the rack in a single layer.
3. Sprinkle the brown sugar and black pepper on the bacon.
4. Bake until brown and crisp, about 30-35 minutes.

Sara's Layered
Pumpkin Cheesecake

This dessert is a smaller version of Sara's restaurant-style cheesecake mentioned in the book.

Gingersnap crust –
   2 cups gingersnap cookie crumbs (about 32 cookies)
   1/4 cup ground walnuts
   1/4 cup butter or margarine, melted

Cheesecake –
   4 8-ounce packages cream cheese, softened
   1 1/2 cups sugar
   4 eggs
   1 cup canned pumpkin (not pumpkin pie mix)
   1 1/2 teaspoons ground ginger
   1 teaspoon ground cinnamon
   1/4 teaspoon ground nutmeg

1. Pre-heat oven to 300º F. Grease a 9-inch spring form pan with cooking spray. Wrap foil around the outside of the pan to catch any leaks.
2. Prepare crust: Mix together cookie crumbs, walnuts, and butter. Press mixture into the bottom of the pan, going up side 1 inch. Bake 8 – 10 minutes. Cool for 5 minutes.
3. In a large bowl, beat the cream cheese until smooth. Add the sugar, and then add the eggs, one at a time, beating until incorporated. Measure out 3 cups of the cheese mixture and spread evenly over the crust.
4. Add pumpkin, ginger, cinnamon, and nutmeg to the remaining cream cheese mixture in the large bowl. Mix with a wire whisk until blended. Spoon pumpkin mixture over the cream cheese mixture in the pan.
5. Bake for about 1 hour and 30 minutes, or until sides look set and

center jiggles just a little when moved.

6. Turn off the oven, open the oven door about 4 inches, and leave cheesecake in the over for 30 more minutes. Remove from oven, set on cooling rack. While cheesecake is still warm, run a knife around the edge. Cool in the pan for 30 minutes. Cover loosely with plastic and refrigerate overnight.

7. When ready to serve, run a knife around the edge again. Carefully remove the spring form. Store leftover cheesecake in the refrigerator.

ABOUT THE AUTHOR

USA Today Bestselling Author **Donna Fasano** has written over 30 romance and women's fiction titles. Her books have won awards and have been publishing in nearly two dozen languages.

Follow her on-line:

Blog:
> http://www.DonnaFasano.com

Facebook:
> https://Facebook.com/DonnaFasanoAuthor

Twitter:
> https://Twitter.com/DonnaFaz

Pinterest:
> https://Pinterest.com/DonnaFaz

Sign up for her newsletter:
> http://mad.ly/signups/110899/join